THE TIME OF HER LIFE

DEBBIE BIRSE

Pen Press Publishers Ltd

First published in Great Britain by
Pen Press Publishers Ltd
The Old School
39 Chesham Road
Brighton BN2 1NB

ISBN: 1-905621-44-2
ISBN13: 978-905621-44-6

Printed and bound in the UK

A catalogue record of this book is available from
the British Library

Cover design by Jacqueline Abromeit
from a painting entitled Mum's Sweet Peas
by Emma Dunbar

Debbie Birse had wanted to write a novel since the age of eight. She studied creative writing with Andrew Davis as part of her English degree at Warwick University, but was side-tracked by working abroad, in publishing and human resources. After her marriage to Tony and the birth of her three sons Michael, Jonathan & Callum, Debbie studied several writing courses at local education centres in west London. She managed to complete half an MA in Writing at Middlesex University, before the latter stages of breast cancer rendered her incapable of continuing with her studies. The first year of the course concentrated on short stories.

Debbie was shortlisted for the Asham Literary prize in 2003 and was a runner up in the Frome Festival short story competition in 2004. Shortly after she died in March 2005, her short story *"From The Window Upstairs"* was read to listeners on BBC Radio Somerset Sound.

The most important people in Debbie's life
were her three boys Michael, Jonathan and Callum
and it is to them that she would have wanted
this book to be dedicated.

CONTENTS

STORIES

POETRY & SHORT PROSE

STORIES

The Time of Her Life

Her doctor didn't tell her, but he told her husband she had six months to two years. Her husband didn't tell her either at first; she returned from being weighed by the nurse and he was saying good-bye to Mr Gordon, her doctor. Hugh's mouth was pinned into a straight line, running parallel with the lines on his forehead and the thin strands of fair hair. If she had spoken to him he would have had to reply, and the tight line of his mouth was holding the rest of his face together. So she stayed silent as her thoughts skidded into each other inside her head. Hugh took her hand on the escalator, a rare gesture between them; they descended to the ground floor of the hospital.

The scent of freesias from the flower shop and hairspray from the hairdresser's replaced the antiseptic, floor polish and that strange, sweet smell of the clinic upstairs. Hugh and Miranda walked through the foyer and the mix of visitors and residents. Grandchildren in buggies and daughters on their lunch hour, carrying coats and looking for the lift. Then the old grey men in tartan dressing gowns, shuffling towards the door, clutching their cigarette packets. Large women in leggings and slippers buying magazines and soap at the newsagent's, down from the wards.

Outside, the sudden August sun glared into their faces. Fumes from the London traffic added to the heavy heat of the air. The old men were smoking on the low wall around the fountain, bony ankles protruding from pyjama trousers, old bones warming in the sun. Two girls were pulling petals from the rose bushes, throwing them into the water with loud squeals. Miranda thought: we have just come out of an airport building, we're in Madrid or Rome for the weekend. She laughed and shivered as the impulsive, happy thought was there, then up against the wall of reality, the reality of her illness. Always there now, blocking such possibilities of happiness. Bubbles of laughter pricked by the sharp edge of her life.

Hugh had turned to her and was now holding both her hands in his. A smile cracked his face, he said, 'Shall we have lunch somewhere? I don't need to go back to the office and Adam won't be out of school for a while.'

Miranda had been watching the spinning petals in the fountain. She released her hands, not liking them held in that way, made a pretence of looking through her bag. (One of her favourites, burgundy leather with a metallic clasp.) What she really wanted was to be alone. Hugh had offered to come with her this time but it upset her routine, her way of handling these visits to the hospital. Miranda underwent tests every three months followed by an appointment with her doctor. Whatever the diagnosis, it was just herself, sometimes a nurse, and the doctor, and everything was contained in that room. The doctor's words, her reaction, her tears and jumping heart. Then she would leave, carrying with her the trembling facts that she would introduce into her life at her own pace. This began in the café across the road, with a cup of tea and writing down Mr Gordon's words in her blue notebook. Then, as long as she liked, just sitting there, pressing the crumbs of her biscuit into the plate.

So now Miranda shrugged her shoulders at Hugh and said, 'Yes, fine, I don't mind.' They turned towards the Italian restaurant, across the road from the hospital. The board outside offered Penne Arrabiata as the day's special, and ten per cent discount for patients with more than twenty stitches.

That evening she waited until Adam had gone to bed and Hugh had gone to his squash.

('Darling, I'd rather stay here with you.'

'No please go, I'm fine.'

'Are you sure you're all right?'

‘Hugh, I’m sure.’

‘You will phone if…’

‘Hugh, just go.’)

Miranda considered a painkiller versus a glass of wine: the latter won. She settled herself on the sofa like a cat in its favourite chair, circling round the cushion, tucking itself in. She kicked off her old loafers – purple suede – and stretched out her long, thin legs in their pink cotton trousers. She loved reds and pinks, the room was a patchwork of her favourite colours. Red wine in the glass swirled against coral walls, raspberry varnished toenails on a rose silk cushion. Her head lay on the armrest, dark hair still spiky from the last chemotherapy but recently tinted a glossy damson colour. Although the August evening was still light, she had drawn the heavy velvet curtains and sealed the room. Miranda reached down for her glass of wine. Now she could deal the cards in her mind, put them into some sort of order before fitting them back into the box.

She had known there was something else she should be told and Hugh could never keep secrets anyway. He must have been persistent as Miranda knew doctors didn’t give this sort of news to relatives anymore. She could see Mr Gordon, his smooth face beneath the sleek, silver hair (like an otter, Miranda had thought at their first meeting) and pale hands folded on her thick hospital file, as he spoke to Hugh. Miranda felt the fear inside her move up from her stomach to her chest. It was like a lift ascending through a shaft of terror within her body. She lay full length on the sofa and, as she had been taught, concentrated on breathing from her diaphragm. The chill reached inside her head, as the images of life without her in it turned over one by one. Adam’s fourteen-year-old rare, sudden hugs, his unbrushed head over a bowl of cereal, this room, her friends, her garden … her eyes creased shut, chilled fingers pressed to the wine glass. She was swimming through freezing water but always, always this tank of fear emptied and she pulled herself up and out of it, every time and even this time, after this latest news. This incredible tide dragged her back to whatever life was left. 'I am not there yet,' Miranda said aloud. She stood up and walked around the room. The bookshelves were full of presents from friends, biographies of miracles and survival. Another shelf contained history texts and foreign language dictionaries, these dated before her illness, after which Miranda couldn't see the point in self-improvement. (She still indulged her love of expensive handbags.) There was a pile of photograph albums and magazines on the floor. Miranda spent hours with old photographs, removing herself from the present. She chose now the latest home interiors magazine. Pages of glossy smiles and bathrooms showed that the world wasn't always so serious; for her it was the best way to finish a day like this.

Later in bed, Miranda curled her arm over Hugh's back. They had slept like bookends for a long time now, each facing the opposite walls of the room. Certainly since she had found out about Hugh's half-hearted attempt at adultery. Tonight she wasn't thinking about whether she still found attractive her husband of fifteen years, a question which kept her from sleeping. She stroked the short fair hair on the back of his neck.

Miranda spent the weekend not answering the telephone, and shopping. She bought new bed linen for herself, in bright red and gold, and an emerald green silk jumper, an extravagant early birthday present for her friend Jenny. These vivid colours worked like a kite tugging against a cloudy sky, pulling her away from flat, grey thoughts. On Monday morning she went to work, assisting the editor in a small publishing office in north London. Her two best friends had tried to persuade her to give up work. Rachel, a City lawyer, said: 'It's not as if it's that exciting, you're always saying how mundane it is.' Jenny, mother of four children, thought she should join a health club instead. But Miranda found the routine soothing: writing the same letters, talking to the same authors and printers, eating her sandwiches on Primrose Hill and buying dinner at the Greek delicatessen on the way back to the tube station. And if she left, what would she do? Moping at home would be dreadful. She had been thinking a lot about her childhood: favourite schoolteachers, holidays with her cousins in Scotland, the clothes and records she bought with her teenage pocket money. God, Miranda thought, wallowing my life away to the tunes of Rod Stewart and Adam Ant. But nor had she any urge to make that trip of a lifetime: to go swimming with dolphins or hiking in the Himalayas. Perhaps if she and Hugh were closer they might watch sunsets together on a Caribbean island, or return to that hotel in Brighton. But after the initial handholding and holding on in the night, they were back alongside rather than with each other, parallel lives walking from bedroom to bathroom and sitting in front of the television. Miranda considered all this in the midday sunshine, overlooking the London skyline from the grassy slopes of Primrose Hill.

On Tuesday morning Miranda received the letter from the hospital with the start date for the next and more aggressive course of chemotherapy. She put down her toast, unable to eat now, turned the lid of the marmalade jar, reading the ingredients. Then, turning towards the kitchen window and against the background of sky, she slotted the new information into her mind's index box. Her coffee was cold by the time the block of fear beneath her ribs had stopped pressing on her breathing.

She waited for it to pass because it always did. Miranda turned back to the kitchen table and the photograph album there. It was lying open at a black and white picture of a square, stone house. Underneath, on the stiff black paper page, someone had written 'Crossways 1930'. This was her father's former home in Scotland where Miranda had spent summer holidays, playing hide and seek and rounders. It was the image she visualised in her relaxation classes. At night she explored the bedrooms leading off the long, dark landing. She pushed her chair back, and by the telephone in the hall she picked up her address book. The telephone rang.

'Hello?'

'Any news?' It was her friend Jenny. The same start to so

many conversations. Miranda would reply either in tears or with flippance. Her thoughts of Crossways had pushed back the tears.

'Oh yes, more chemotherapy, more throwing up, back to the baseball hats and head scarves. Just as I've achieved this perfect colour on my hair, too.'

'Oh God, Miranda, not again. You poor thing – can I come over?'

'Actually, I'm all right, thanks, Jenny. I've got things to do, I must call someone, I'll speak to you later?'

Miranda hung up after saying good-bye and turned the pages of the address book. She dialled a number.

'Hello?'

'Hello, Aunt Dora?'

'This is Dora, who's that?'

'Aunt Dora, it's Miranda.'

'Miranda? Miranda! How lovely, how are you, dearie?'

Miranda felt a smile lift her whole face. Through the warm, Scottish voice she saw Crossways and the tall figure of her elderly aunt at a downstairs window.

'I'm OK, I'm sorry I haven't called before. How are you?'

'Fine, grand, busy with grandchildren. Did you know I'm a great-grandmother now?'

Miranda sat on the bottom stair and listened to news of her cousins and their families. She had not seen her aunt since her father's funeral five years earlier. Aunt Dora was his older sister.

'Now Miranda, why don't you come and see us all?'

When Miranda had hung up and stretched from her position on the stairs, she was still smiling. 'At least twenty minutes not thinking about It.' The edges of her life which kept curling up had been pressed down again. She went to make more coffee.

That evening Miranda was back on the sofa. A Radio 4 play had replaced Rod Stewart. Her hair on the pink cushion was now an even deeper damson colour. An earlier act of defiance in the bathroom... 'Up yours, Mr Gordon, my last few days of gorgeous hair.' Loose clumps of red hair on her new pillowcases: she shut her eyes to seal this image from her mind. Miranda took a deep breath, a sip of wine, and lay back to take her thoughts away from the hospital and instead to Crossways. She saw Dora at the front door, welcoming her. Miranda followed her aunt up the stairs into a bedroom, and put her suitcase on the bed. Then she was lying on the bed, a pale yellow bedspread on the dark wooden frame. There were fresh flowers on the dressing table, branches and white blossom latticed the window. She could hear her aunt downstairs, talking with one of her grandchildren. This family of hers was like her old sheepskin at the back of the wardrobe. Rarely worn now but comforting to know it was there. Unlike her immediate family: Adam her son was more like an undergarment worn all year round, next to her skin, even when it was too warm. And Hugh? From the distance of Crossways Miranda knew Hugh no longer fitted.

Miranda sat up on the sofa. She was going to sort herself out at Crossways. She finished her wine and threw a cushion up against the shelves of miracle stories. But they had all really happened.

'No, I'm not there yet.'

Howard's Women

I didn't like Helen when I met her ten years ago, and I didn't expect to like her now. Of course, she had good reason to dislike me, not only taking her husband but also her place in the kitchen, on the sofa, in the bath (any one of the six in the house). She moved out of Greenacres, stood at the front door waiting for the taxi with her Burberry luggage packed - and I squeezed past her, into the hall and closed the door behind me.

Greenacres. Beautiful Greenacres, Howard's Elizabethan manor on the South Downs. Paid for with the earnings from a run of successful plays in the West End. And shared with me for the last ten years. Until last week, when I received Howard's letter.

Helen and I are meeting to discuss Howard. (His name is Roger Howard but everyone calls him Howard, except for his American agent who greets him with 'Hey, Howie!') Howard would just love it if he knew: two women arranging a lunch just to talk about him.

I didn't know anywhere to eat in London now: Helen chose a restaurant off St James', somewhere with a dialling code for a name. 'It's post-modern deconstructed cuisine,' she had said. I could just imagine the place – the zinc bar, high ceiling and whirring fans, skinny waiters in black and white. And those narrow, pale wooden chairs with heart shaped seats: like sitting on a child's bicycle. I could feel the dents in my buttocks already.

What does one wear to meet one's ex-husband's first wife? I chose purple: my favourite Hobbs jacket, with matching kitten heels. I've got good legs for a woman with hips like dodgem-car bumpers. Admiring the curves of my body, Howard used to call them his very own ripe mangoes, peaches, pears. Ten years ago he had chosen my luscious bowl of fruit over Helen's fancily packaged dried apricots. I must remember this when I see her.

I arrived early in London, walked down Piccadilly and into Green Park. It was a fresh April morning, although it struggled with the bus diesel fumes. I wished I could buy a Prêt a Manger sandwich and a Coke, then go and sit in one of the green and white striped deckchairs in the park. I envied all the people doing just this, on their lunch hour, in the company of people they liked.

'Brasserie 110' was just as I had imagined, down to the waiters with ridiculous white aprons, like loincloths. Yes, Mrs Howard is here, I was told. Yes, but he left *that* Mrs Howard for *this* Mrs Howard, I told the narrow black hips as I followed them through the restaurant. We passed table after table of white cloths, white dishes and glossy coiffured heads. There was Helen. She sat at a corner table, on her heart shaped bottom, no doubt. She got up slowly, long legs stretching in flesh coloured fishnet tights, coffee coloured leather skirt and white silk T-shirt. A long, glamorous cigarette. Her fine red hair was pinned up, her neck a slender piece of Lladro china. I felt like a big, shiny aubergine.

'Hello, Helen, you look nice as always.'

'Hello, Kath, you've not changed either.'

We sat opposite each other; Helen sipped her sparkling water. I unbuttoned my jacket, picked up my napkin and screwed it into a ball in my lap. Put my hands on the table. I was wearing my emerald ring: its stone the size of a wine gum, a gift from Howard on our honeymoon.

The waiter was still there, shiny black eyes, like olives, on and all over Helen, hands sweating on the laminated menus.

'Any wine for you, ladies?'

'Yes, please,' I said, and he handed me the list. 'Helen, would you like some wine?'

'I don't drink.'

'I hope you eat,' I said. Helen did not smile. Her dislike of me floated there in her clear green eyes.

I ordered a bottle of Merlot and reached for a bread roll. I always eat when I'm bothered about something. I ate two whole cheesecakes the night of Howard's and my last argument. Helen watched as I buttered the bread, counting the fat content of each swipe of my knife.

'How's life then, Helen, are you working?'

'A little.'

'Still gardening?'

'I potter.' She spoke slowly, as though conversation with me was hardly worth bothering with. The waiter brought the bottle of wine. He watched Helen's breasts instead of the bottle, the cork popped with a jerk and drops of red spat onto his white shirt. He filled my glass quickly and left.

I took a large mouthful of wine and felt better.

'Well, I've discovered a bit of a flair for interior design,' I said. 'I've been designing friends' bathrooms. And I've redecorated every room at Greenacres –'

I didn't mean this as a dig, but it came out like one. Whatever my feelings for Helen, Greenacres had been her home for ten years. I adored the house, she probably had as well.

'Is the sitting room still rather dark?' Helen asked.

'Actually no, we've completely changed the lighting and –'

'We? Don't tell me darling Howard changed a light bulb?'

'That's not what I –'

'And the bedrooms, all rather pokey for such a large house. Howard used to bang his head on the dressing room ceiling. Careful, Kath, you're spilling your wine.'

I had taken several mouthfuls of the Merlot as I was getting sweaty and cross. Luckily my jacket was Merlot colour. I didn't feel like defending Howard but I didn't like Greenacres being criticised. I helped myself to more bread and thought of my gorgeous stone and mango en suite bathroom, finished only last week.

Helen was smiling, her thin, elegant arms stretched out on the table. I was trying to contain my anger, had tucked it firmly into my handbag, but the clasp was in danger of snapping. I took a deep breath.

'OK, Helen, let's forget the small talk. Let's talk about Howard's letters. But I'm starving, can we order some food first?'

I cheered up reading the menu; caramelised onion tartlet, white bean and Parmesan soup, a timbale of avocado with a tranche of wild pear, conchiglie with tarragon. Things drizzled in something and marinated in something else. And there was my favourite: garlic prawns.

Helen tossed her head and the waiter arrived immediately. I wanted to ask him what hair gel he used – my own black curls never looked so sleek.

'Well, ladies?'

'Helen, what are you having?'

'A side order of grated red cabbage to start, then a green salad – no dressing.'

'Is that it? OK – can I have the garlic prawns, please? And – oh, they all sound so yummy – the pesto and duck pate stuffed chicken. Thank you.'

'With French fries, Madam?' The waiter flicked a smile across to Helen, then turned back to me. He was sizing up a delicate string of linguine lunching with a plate of gnocchi dumplings.

'Just the vegetables, thank you.'

We sat back in our chairs, returned to our corners. Another deep breath and a gulp of wine. Helen was texting from her mobile, probably to a fellow grated cabbage eater. So I indulged in reminiscing about Greenacres.

I had fallen in love with Howard before I saw Greenacres. He was witty, handsome, he was flattering, he ran his hand through that floppy blond hair a lot. Which I then enjoyed doing for him, on the sofa, on our evenings back at his or my flat. Howard's flat was in the Barbican, and he just happened to mention over dinner one night that he owned another property: 'my old place in the country.' I realise now he was waiting for Helen to vacate herself and her belongings before taking me there. I had to wait several weekends. Then, one luscious red and gold Sunday afternoon in October, we drove out of London and through the South Downs, along perfect Sussex lanes between hedges the colour of cartloads of apples. We turned into a long, gravelled driveway and there it was - Greenacres: a gabled, half-timbered, leaded windowed manor house. I had been swigging from a bottle of sparkling water. In my astonishment at the house the water was splattered onto the MG's windscreen.

'My God, Howard, you never said. How can you bear to live in London when you've got this? Goodness, and it comes complete with old retainers and tugging forelocks.' An aged gardener was smiling from his wheelbarrow, caught in a slanting late afternoon sunbeam.

I was definitely in love now. The boot room was bigger than my entire flat. After making love that night, with the shutters open onto the moon and the dew sprinkled lawn, I crept along the gallery and down the central staircase. I only needed a broderie anglaise cap and a candle. I hummed Greensleeves. In the kitchen fridge I found some pork pie and munched this on the bottom stair in the hall.

When I moved in a few weeks later, as Mrs Howard number two-to-be, I couldn't wait for Howard to go up to London for his work. I had always carried out most of my research work from my flat, so could and would happily continue at Greenacres. But for days the laptop stayed in the oak chest in the hall. I floated alone around the house and garden, from the library to the orchard.

Our food arrived. Helen sifted through the grated cabbage: little red splinters on a large white plate. I picked up, then put down my fork. I ate the plump, pink, buttery prawns with my fingers. I saw the wrinkle of horror on Helen's face, so I licked my oily fingers, one by one, slurped more garlic butter then more wine.

'OK, Helen, so what did Howard say in his letter to you?'

'Just that he's leaving you, and making a fresh start.'

Helen raised an eyebrow languidly across the table.

'Of course there's a girl involved, although he didn't give details,' she said. 'But I've heard that she's rather pretty.'

I'd heard this too, from several so-called friends. I took two large mouthfuls of the scrumptious rich pate, and said,

'Yes, but what else did he say about Greenacres?'

'Oh yes, that part. He said that the house is yours and mine.'

This was what Howard had written to me, too. 'You sort it out between yourselves,' he had said.

I said, 'Are we going to need lawyers?'

'Do you want to stay at Greenacres?'

'Why, do you want it?'

Helen twirled a piece of cucumber on her fork, like a parasol. I looked down and attacked my chicken, dreading her answer.

'Is he in the States already?' Helen asked.

'Yes, New York. Kandi – with a K and an i – he's designing sets for his new play. She's 22, and a blonde. She also wants lots of babies. Howard says he's up for it.'

'Bastard.'

'Yes.'

I refilled my wine glass and, without thinking, poured some into Helen's glass. She nodded at me, and took a sip.

I thought of my newly painted Turkish Delight walls in the bathroom, the subtle tones of Whisper Grey in the hall. Was Helen remembering the wisteria around the leaded windows, the lime tree walk, the oak gallery and stairs?

'So, unless you want to move back, you want me to sell it, I suppose?' I knocked my fork onto the floor as I thought I might cry, which turns my face into a wrinkled nectarine.

'Of course I don't want to move back to Greenacres.' The wine had taken the chill from her eyes.

The waiter came to clear away. The plates clattered in the tension at the table. He left without speaking, doing a shimmy between tables, like a Brazilian footballer through a sluggish defence.

'Helen, can I ask you: why did you move out? It was Howard who left you.'

'Oh, Sussex wasn't me. All those church flowers and dumpy women and garden fetes. And friends arriving for the weekend and expecting to be fed. Howard offered to buy me a flat in London and I jumped at it.'

'If I stay – and, well, I do love Greenacres – I could pay you, or bloody Howard could pay – ' I had a thought. 'Or I could sell the field behind the orchard wall. The farmer next door would be delighted.'

'What, that cross-eyed man with the leer?'

'You remember him with affection, then?'

We both laughed.

'You know something, Helen? You had the best of him – Howard. Then I got him recycled, and now, well – he's not biodegradable, he'll just rot very slowly. And honestly, I could put up with all the scratching and the preening, when his body was worth preening. Oh – and that gorgeous blond hair.'

'Yes, gorgeous blond hair: Robert Redford in *The Way We Were*.'

'Oh yes. But now – his stomach folds over his belt like calzone – and there's not a lot of hair left.'

We toasted Howard's balding head.

'He was best drunk young, Helen. The American tart is welcome to the dregs. I don't suppose you'd like to share a dessert?'

Mother Love

It is Nina's sixth birthday today and she is having a party. All her friends from school have arrived, giggling and clutching multicoloured wrapped presents. Nina has pink hairslides in her straight fair hair, and pink cheeks as she opens the door and sees her friends. They have games, music, a Barbie cake, balloons.

I know about the balloons because I saw them tied to the gate as I drove past – so there is a party. But it is my youngest daughter's sixth birthday and I don't know the name of her best friend or even if she likes Barbie.

Nina smelt of warm earth when she was born. I held her soft warmth close, and inhaled that smell. Her two sisters came to visit, bringing the December cold in with them. Lindy and Jess wore red coats and red mittens, and took turns at sitting on the hard, green vinyl chair, holding their baby sister. Little mothers already, at two and four years old. Who brought them to the hospital? I could hardly see Dave by then, he had grown fainter with the birth of each of the girls, a shadow falling across the hospital bed. Ten years before, Dave had thick yellow hair, a loud laugh, and we raced to Brighton on his red and silver motorbike. If he was there on that visit, I didn't notice him.

Nina was six months old, the first time I left. As their father faded, the girls and the walls of the house pressed forward. I knew I was disappearing too. My arms and legs had no weight. I bit my arm and there were no teeth marks. I cut my hand with a knife and felt nothing. I wrapped a tea towel round my hand, picked up my handbag and walked out of the front door. The first time I left.

So I hadn't seen Nina as I drove past, and they have replaced the old metal gate with a wooden one, painted blue. I am not living there as their mother but some parts of me are still in that house. Grandma Joyce, Dave's mother, is cooking the girls' tea and brushing their hair, but fragments of me have slipped down the side of the cooker, in between the bathroom tiles, under the pillows on their beds. As a girl, I had shaped faces on my bedroom wallpaper out of the spaces in the pink and white flower print; mermaids and princesses from trailing green leaves and pink petals. Do my daughters see princesses, or do they see *my* face between the rabbits and puppies on their wall? Fluffy ears becoming my long curly hair, the round animal faces lengthening into my face. Can they remember my face? My hair is short and straight now, I combed it after parking the car here. This is my brother's old car, to get me out and about, he said. But I only use it to come and sit here. There is a December fog outside, and inside, the car has steamed up with my memories.

I was gone for just two days that first time I left. It was a summer's evening, and mild; I walked in the amber, late afternoon sunlight, and through the grainy evening darkness. I must have had my purse in my bag, as I had a brown plastic cup of tea and an iced doughnut in an unknown park, in the morning. The bench was beside a wire dustbin into which I tore the empty cup. Pigeons came to stab at the crumbs brushed from my jeans when I stood up. I crossed the two bridges over the river in the town centre many times, always in the same direction. I didn't stop to look from the bridge as I didn't want my thoughts to become caught up in the rush of green water below.

I arrived back home, and stood for a second in the hall on my own. First came the thick smells of the house: fried bacon from the kitchen, wet clothes on the radiator, that dense family smell of plasticine and Ready Brek. Then Dave, hesitating before he hugged me, holding on to me because I started crying. But I cried because, walking across those bridges, I had seen my old Dave, a solid bulk in a biker's jacket. I couldn't feel his arms and only saw them around me in the hall mirror. (I did think: that's good, my reflection is still there.)

The girls were sat in a row on the sofa watching television, Lindy, the oldest, holding baby Nina. I dropped to my knees in front of them. Lindy and Jess turned their heads slowly from the screen and shuffled forward into my arms. I could feel them, their arms and legs around me, their warm breath on my neck and little fingers in my hair… pulling me back.

Later, Dave and I sat over tinfoil takeaway containers and cans of beer at the kitchen table. He had called the police to say I had returned, and they were sending someone to talk to me in the morning. I watched Dave's fork move through his curry. Between mouthfuls he said, 'Tell me, Michelle, talk to me. You can't just do that, you know. I mean, Christ the girls …'

I don't know if I had spoken since I got back. Did I ask if he had managed with Nina's bottles, Jess' tantrums, had he gone to work, what had his mother said? All that I should have said, how I felt in that house, was wrapped up too tightly, packed down too far inside. As I scraped rice into the dustbin I remembered the green wrought-iron bench in the park, and the space I had felt around me then. Up to the sky and then out to the edges of the park. Until the pigeons came pecking at my feet and I got up to go home.

I stayed through the summer but the house moved in closer during the dark afternoons of winter. I left several times, and often, during the winter. I spent a night in a hostel, one night in the doorway of a shoe shop: I forget the other places. I never went to my brother's flat in the next town along the river, nor to the mothers from the girls' school, although Dave always phoned them. He had stopped calling the police.

There was no pattern to my leaving, I would lose my shape in the house and have to get out to find it and pull it over me again. I was a coat hanger in a set of clothes. I saw my body move up the stairs once, and heard a door closing. At night the bedroom ceiling hung just above my face, the wardrobe leaned over the end of the bed. I would hear Jess crying out in her sleep and her cries would coil round in my ears, round and round, long after her room was silent again.

I was not a bad mother, I was calm and patient with them. They wanted me in their dressing up games, winding glass beads round my neck, wrapping old lace shawls around me, threading ribbons in my hair with tangling fingers. They cut thick, uneven slices of cake, then clambered into my lap to feed me, giggling at the crumbs in my hair and on my face. I can remember Dave being there in pieces only; his face at the table, his legs in front of the television. We shared a bed but, as he was disappearing like me, the pillows were undented in the morning, there was no warmth left behind beneath the quilt.

Grandma Joyce visited with her shepherd's pies; vests and tights for the girls and sleeping tablets for me. Her brown cardiganned bulk, and efficient washing up, quietened the house, and sometimes the walls stayed back when she was in the room. It finally happened after one of her visits. I was closing the front door, Dave and the girls were dancing to the radio in the kitchen. I turned to the hall mirror. It was a heavy, ornate mirror from my parents' bedroom, I used to brush my hair in front of it with my mother watching from the bed. But now my hair was not there, I was not there, I could see only the coats hanging up behind me. My hand was a translucent glove, I held it up to the mirror. Nothing. I knew I had at last disappeared.

I left and did not return after that. At the end of one day I found the hostel I had stayed in three winters before, and a few times after that, climbed under a navy woollen blanket and lay still for a long time. I got up one morning, bought some writing paper at a newsagent's and wrote to Dave that I had left for good. Another morning I caught a coach that followed the river to the town where I grew up. I knocked on the door of our old house but there was no answer. I found somewhere to stay, a small bedsit above a launderette, then later I read a card in a window: "Shop Assistant Required." I started selling sweets and cigarettes behind a counter. The beige walls in my room were stained and ugly but they stayed at the edges of the room. I could feel my hair when I combed it, feel the coins in my hand in the shop. I had appeared again, I could be seen from the outside. But inside I was hollow. Through my head and my body there was nowhere for thoughts of the girls to rest. Their images floated inside the empty shell and found nowhere to take a hold. I learnt from my brother that Grandma Joyce had moved in and stayed.

After about nine months in the shop, there were some mornings when I got up and it was different. I opened the window and looked across to the river behind the shops across the street. I could feel the sun warm my face or smell the fresh, wet air when it rained. On these mornings I would wash my hair, choose the pale blue of my three shirts, eat a piece of toast with my cup of tea before going to work. I saw which window displays had been changed in the High Street and which cakes the bread shop was selling. On these mornings Will was making his regular visit to the shop, restocking the wine gums and the chocolate bars. Will Wright is a sales representative for Cornershop Confectionery UK, and lives in the north of England. He always shook my hand, even when Maureen the owner was in the shop with me. He is a small man but his hands are large, and the affection of that handshake would stay with me all day. Will is short and balding, he looks untidy in his pale grey suit. But he would lean against the counter, gesturing with his hands as he spoke, his easy manner and Yorkshire accent underpinning his conversation with gentle humour. Will's visits started to run into my lunch hour, we bought sausage rolls at the bread shop to eat by the river. Side by side I am taller than him, but his warmth filled along the length of the wooden bench. The emptiness inside began to fill up. One lunchtime, a warm April midday, I was watching the sun glaze the river with its light. And I told Will that I had a family with whom I no longer lived, that I had children. Will nodded, his kind eyes turned from the river to look at me, he removed the sandwich wrapper I had been tearing into strips and rolled it in his hands. He waited for me to say something else. I told him the names and ages of the girls. Again he nodded and waited. When I stayed silent, he turned back to the river, his arm along the back of the bench.

The birthday candles must have been blown out by now. I am still parked around the corner so I did not see the cluster of excited friends going home, presents exchanged for party bags. This is the last time I can do this, come back like this. Will has asked me to live with him and his sister in the house they inherited and now share, along with the occasional lodger when the roof needs repairing, a widowed sister who sometimes stays, two or three longhaired cats. He has described the dark Victorian house in Yorkshire, the freshly painted yellow front door and the overgrown garden, with the same affection he attaches to everything. As I sit here, boxed in by the December fog, I imagine a room I might inhabit in that house. I see burgundy walls, a white bedspread, a walnut dressing table, an ornate mirror like my mother's. And then I see photographs of Lindy, Jess and Nina on the dressing table. I have never carried pictures of them in my purse, nor displayed any above the fireplace in my bedsit. But now they are there on the dressing table. I can feel myself breathing in and out, long, deep breaths, filling the shell beneath my rib cage. I will brush my hair at the dressing table, watched by my reflection and the framed images of the girls.

I turn on the engine, the sudden blast of heat de-mists the windscreen, the headlamps cut through the thick fog. I drive past the shop where we used to buy fish and chips and take the road back along the river.

From The Window Upstairs

Sometimes I wake up and find myself somewhere else. I'm not here in my bed, lying next to Mark, with Chloe asleep next door. This is a place that hangs in my memory, like a picture passed so often, you no longer see the shapes and colours. I'm in a dark hall and my hand is held tightly. Although I can't see him, it's my father holding my hand. It's that first time he took me there.

The dark is heavy, my breathing mingles with the dark's own breath. I am five years old and I am afraid. I smell fur coats, a fire burning, and roses, too: this fresh smell tints the dark like a lit match. Tugged down the hall, my free hand finds the edges of the first door. This is Aunt Alice's room, the door is closed. The next door is closed, too: this is my grandmother's study. At the foot of the stairs my hand is released. I am alone now. My bare feet press on the cold of the stone floor. At the end of the hall is the kitchen where warm light and my grandmother's baking are just inside the door. But the pull of this dream is upwards, my hand slides up the banister rail as I walk up the stairs. And it is lighter now. I pass all the bedroom doors along the corridor, and up another staircase.

The light comes from a round window on the second landing. The panes of glass are set deep into the wall: a giant's fist has knocked the hole through from the outside. I look down into my grandmother's garden, the vegetable patch, down to the cedar tree at the end. I sit in the curve of the window and wait, as I always do in this dream. But this morning is different.

This slip of time passes. The radio is on and I can hear water running in the bathroom. Chloe will be in soon. I stay for a while on the pillows.

I was left there for about a month, the first time. The next time my father took me, I stayed for five years. My grandmother made a hedgehog birthday cake for my tenth birthday, with Matchmaker spikes and a marshmallow nose. A red and silver bicycle stood by the front door, from my father's visit that morning. He stayed for a cup of tea and just long enough to leave the smell of his damp overcoat hanging in the hall, with the label on the handlebars.

Evie and Aunt Alice looked after me together. (My father called her Evie so I did – never Grandmother.) Alice died a couple of years ago. She was short and heavy, but with dainty feet: she used to dance alone in her room.

'Isn't she a bonny girl?' These were Alice's first words to me; I was leaning against my father on the doorstep. It was the first time I'd heard 'bonny' said like that. I am built more like my aunt than my grandmother. Evie was – still is – tall, straight backed in her long, narrow skirts. The lines in Evie's face were crevices cut close together, like the contours on the maps in my school atlas. Alice's features were the drystone walls of the fields around our house: her broad cheeks, solid nose. She was vain of her hands, rubbing cream into them at the breakfast table, wearing rubber gloves to polish my school shoes. Her fingertips were as smooth as olives. Alice had wavy, reddish hair, the patch of colour on a robin. I drew her head over the piano keys, colouring in her hair with a bundle of strokes: red, orange, brown. My grandmother's hair was straight and grey – the colour was in her blue eyes. Her fingertips were walnut shells. I drew her in the kitchen, her glasses perched on the kettle spout, her hands twisting lids onto raspberry jam.

'Your mother always had a pencil in her hand.'

'Tell me again about her rabbit – and her friend Sally.' Evie described her daughter's childhood to me as she moved about the kitchen. I drew pictures of my mother and Sally, playing under the cedar tree.

Evie and Alice looked after the house and me between them. Like the dealing out in the card games I played with Evie at the kitchen table. 'One for you and one for me.' Evie cooked, gardened, looked after my clothes and my homework - taught me to sit quietly during a radio play. Alice washed and cleaned in the house, and taught me to play the piano and about life's unpredictability. My piano lessons might be scale after scale, peering at the music in her dimly lit room. Or she would set a Mozart sonata in front of me and nod her head for me to begin. Sometimes she would sit down alongside me and bump me along so she could play. Light, delicate Chopin waltzes that matched her small, dancing feet. Alice collected glass ornaments, and they would shimmer and chink together in the cabinet on the wall.

When I came home from school, I would go to find Alice in her room. She might be cutting out pictures from magazines, or just sitting still on the piano stool. Once she was eating rose petals. She would ask, 'Did Molly have salad cream sandwiches today?' She would rummage under a cushion and hold out a box of toffees.

In the kitchen, Evie would give me an apple and ask, 'How did you do in your spelling test? Did you remember "appreciation"?'

These exchanges with my aunt and grandmother were the stiles across the field of my childhood. I had been riding the new bicycle for a few months when my father took me back to live with him, and with Shona, his new wife-to-be.

Chloe is in bed with me now. She is telling me about her dreams, but I have not let go of mine yet. For the first time in my dream this morning, when I had sat in the round window and looked out, I had seen someone sitting under the blue grey cedar tree. I could not see her face as she was looking down, drawing in a sketchbook. But I recognised the golden hair of my mother from the many photographs at Evie's house, and from the one in the drawer of my father's desk.

'Chloe poppet, do you want to go and clean your teeth with Daddy?'

Evie used to read out my mother's letters at teatime, once a month, sometimes less often. As though, once a month, a place was set for her at the tea table. The airmail envelope sat on top of Evie's mending basket on the dresser all day. Sometimes I picked it up during the day and smelt the blue foreign paper. I saw my mother painting at an easel under the Eiffel Tower. Her letters began, 'Dear Mother, Alice and Katie.' She didn't know I was Kate by then. My mother wrote of art galleries, street cafes, the parks with long, white paths and neat lawns; the long hours of sunshine. She ate breakfast outside and had shutters at her bedroom window. I sliced the top of my boiled egg, the yolk streaking down the smooth brown shell. I saw the sunshine in my mother's long golden hair. Jardin des Tuilleries, Rive Gauche, Musee Picasso. There were postcards, from Perpignan and Provence, then Naples and Amalfi. She never referred to my father or their divorce. Aunt Alice stirred sugar into her teacup and clattered the spoon in the saucer as her mother read.

'Are France and Italy prettier than Yorkshire?' I once asked. Aunt Alice pulled on her rubber gloves and started washing the floor.

'They're different,' Evie said. Alice opened the back door and emptied her bucket at the drain outside. On the back page of my school exercise book I drew the open door and the slope of the hills, the humped back of a sleeping animal. I thought of my mother drawing the sea. Much later I learnt from Evie that my mother had worked in bars and washed dishes. Someone in Nice once asked for a portrait of his wife.

One of my mother's letters arrived on the day of my accident. After Evie had read the letter, I had finished my homework and was playing with my friend Dan in his father's barn. His family lived on the farm just down the road. Our game of stuffing handfuls of straw down each other's T-shirts had turned into jumping from the huge pile of hay. Dan's father swore afterwards that he hadn't left the pitchfork lying on the ground in the barn. I fell through the hay, banged my head on the wooden handle and put my hand down hard on the metal spikes. Evie and Alice were there when I regained consciousness. I heard them squabbling over who would drive to the hospital and who would hold the tea towel over the hole in my hand.

'At least it's her left hand.'

'Be quiet, Alice.'

Of course I was fine. I had a tetanus jab, a dressing on my head and twelve stitches across the top of my palm. I slept and dreamt about my mother winding a bandage around my hand. I woke up feeling grumpy with everyone.

'When can I go to Paris?'

My father arrived from London with a five hundred-piece puzzle of Big Ben. He drove me back to Evie's house and stayed the night, sleeping on the sofa in Evie's study.

Evie told me she had decided not to read my mother's letters aloud anymore, but would leave them for me on the dresser. I looked at the postmarks but didn't open the blue envelopes.

My father brought Shona with him on his next visit. The three of us had lunch in a hotel. Shona chose the same ice cream sundae as me: strawberry and vanilla, with strawberry sauce. She told me she was from Ireland and grew up in a house just like Evie's. She asked me to be her bridesmaid and let me draw a picture of my dress. We chose the material in Leeds, pale yellow silk, and afterwards had another ice cream sundae.

I stopped drawing my mother's hair and the easel on the Mediterranean beach. I painted the sea once after a day trip to Whitby. It was a wet day, the waves were dull greys and greens.

At art college I preferred dark landscapes to the blocks of primary colour painted by the other students. Mark and I went to Dublin for our honeymoon, although Mark had at first suggested Paris. After Chloe was born, I used to sketch a little whilst she slept in the afternoon. Until the day she climbed out of her cot and cut her forehead on the skirting board. I stopped drawing after that. My mother had died in a car accident when I was fourteen.

It's time to get up. Mark must have helped Chloe to dress because I can hear them in the kitchen. Mark has drawn back one of the bedroom curtains; I'm lying in a pool of sunlight and am still within the glow of my dream. For the first time, under the tree in Evie's garden, I saw my mother drawing.

I pick up the pencil from my bedside table. I open the back cover of the paperback there and draw the long hair, the branches of the cedar tree, her arm at right angles to the sketch pad. Then I draw an outline of Chloe's face. I am pleased with the likeness. I will shade in the delicate red hair later, the light blue eyes of her great grandmother.

'Your mother always had a pencil in her hand.'

My Side of the Story

This is the first time it's happened, but they aren't going to believe that. I would like someone to open the window for me but no one will – and I can hardly do it myself. There are two tubes hanging from every limb, I am an octopus held down on the ironed white seabed. My nose and mouth are just at water level, bubbles of air skimming across the surface as I grab hold of the next breath. Arms and legs are pinned but my thoughts sail across the green tank.

This is how I see myself in this closed green room, with a guard at the door. The pain, too, just grazes the surface, a scum of light green. The circles of pain widen just before the nurse comes to adjust the drip, and then I remember the knife... the slit between my ribs, as smooth as opening an envelope. After the nurse has left, the hurt is just a stain on the surface again. I sleep most of the time.

Beyond the tide of this room is my life before. I see buses, I am at the bus stop going to work. It's wet and the wind flicks the rain like paint off a paintbrush. I see children's feet running, a café, a shoe shop, a flower shop. Red petals are wet, they are splashes of blood in the rain. Further down the road is my house. There are dirty cups and plates in the living room; the broken lamp has not been fixed. I do not open the kitchen door and I don't go upstairs. I walk back along the road, my wet hair hanging like snapped rubber bands. I can only feel this, I cannot see myself there: I have been ripped from the picture. The rooms of my house are only pasted onto the picture. The dried glue is cracked, now flaking off.

I have tried smiling at the large nurse with the gaps in her teeth. Smiling lying flat is just another cut across the body. She doesn't smile, she lifts a tube, wraps the Velcro sleeve around my arm for my blood pressure. Her teeth and eyebrows are a dragon's, I can see the scales down her spine as she leaves.

I am able to speak but the liquid in the tubes dilutes the meaning. My words are clearer when the pain increases; I sharpen my words on the flint of pain and try then to ask my questions. Please can you open the window? What have you told my mum and dad? *Is he still alive?*

They have sat me up now and two of the tubes have gone. The room has green walls, the tank of water lapping at my brain has drained away. My eyes are on the level with the windowsill and I can see the roofs of high-rise flats, the lids on all the lives below. A doctor sat on my bed today and asked me how I was. I didn't answer because I didn't know. He clicked the nib of his pen in and out in time to my breathing. Afterwards a policeman and policewoman came in. He stood at the end of the bed, blocking out the light. She was young and quite pretty, and looked round the room before looking at me. There was nothing for her to see, we both knew why there were no flowers or boxes of chocolates. She sat on the bed, like the doctor had done. She had that fine, blonde hair, a bit like my sister's. Mine is oil yellow. They have washed my body but not my hair; the yellow pool stains the pillow.

'Kay, we want you to tell us what happened.' She must be about my age, I wonder if she is married.

'Kay, the doctor says you are getting better. I know you can hear me, please tell me what happened.'

But I pretended I couldn't speak and I closed my eyes. If I had let them have my bit of strength then, I would have had none left now for myself. And I need to work it out. The doctor had said the knife punctured my lung and splintered my thigh bone, but that I am going to be all right. I have lost a lot of blood. I felt nothing when the knife was going in and, although I saw the wipes of blood, it was inside my head I felt red, hot and wet, seeping inside with the noise. The room was red with the noise of my screaming and his screaming. He was there in bits, his hand, a sleeve; the face of the liar.

It *was* the first time it happened.

But what about everything else? Everybody on Martin's side. Everybody loves Martin. They fall for his f…..g Irish charm, just like I did. Martin's black curly hair you want to coil in your fingers. The mouth forever curled into a smile.

'Aren't you the loveliest thing I've seen all day?' That's what he said, the first time we met. Then just waited, because his smile had all night.

'Are you having a drink, or what?' That was me, behind the bar.

'I'll take what.'

'Cheeky sod, come on, what you having?'

'I think you know what I'd like.'

'Right, I'm going to make a guess, pour you a Guinness, then serve someone else.'

'You do just that. But I'm going to sit right here with my drink and wait for your beautiful blue eyes to look back at me.'

His hand stroked mine as he took the glass. Last time I felt that hand it was fisted into one of my eyes. I think he was smiling even then, and panting like we were screwing. Blood smeared his mouth like lipstick.

The police have gone, although the guard is still at the door. The large nurse is here, she is silent, hiding her ugly teeth. She doesn't want my sympathy and will give me none of hers. The pain in my leg is a sheet of metal, hammered flat. But the nurse holds a needle into the tube and the pain will soon slide off my leg, just as my memory will slide beyond reach. My ribs will become a bundle of hollow logs, loosely tied, bumping each other as they float down the green river. I will sleep.

I dream about our honeymoon. The wooden hut on the white beach. The fan on the ceiling and the bedclothes on the floor. We're on the bed, I can see Martin's face but my face is not there. I feel myself trying to sit up in my sleep now, to look for my face. It's there, under the pillow, there is blood under the pillow. And then there is a face beneath Martin's but it's not mine. It's not me with Martin, it's her.

I wake up and it's dark. The tubes swing as my hands creep to the edges of the bed. I am here and I am alone. The pain in my body lets me bang my anger into shape. Why have my parents not come to visit me? Why has nobody asked me about all the times he left me?

Because it *was* the first time I did this, the first time I picked up a knife, but not the first time he left me. They know nothing about his sneaking off, not coming back from work, not coming back at night. No one believed me, he would even hold my hand when we went out. We still met Mum and Dad in the pub on Thursday nights. They loved him.

'Your Martin, he's a scream.' My Mum drank the gins he bought her and told him about the women she worked with. He called her Ma.

'But Ma, I bet you're the life and soul of the place. Pop's a very lucky man.'

'Your husband's a fine feller. His jokes, he's a real killer.' Dad returning from the snooker table with Martin. Martin let him win every time. And he meant it all, this was all for real. It was at home that he changed. At first, he just teased me about my untidiness and clumsiness, or when I stayed in bed all Saturday. I was a flat glass of beer on the table next to his fizzing bottle, just opened. I couldn't keep up with his energy, the fizz in that bottle, Martin's clanging, optimistic view of life that rang out every morning when he awoke.

'Come on, Kay, we're going out – yer going to change that blouse? That pink one I got you looks great – shows off your eyes.'

I'm looking out of the window at the grey dusk. And then, like a child ripping off the corner of a wrapped birthday present, just to take a peek, I tear a corner in that evening, the one they all want me to remember for them. The night he said he was going to leave.

But I knew, oh I knew, because her smell was already on him, the smell of another woman's life. Her food, her fingernails. I had slept most of the afternoon and had washed my hair. My doctor had signed me off work for another two weeks. I was standing at the kitchen window, it was dark outside. I was chopping mushrooms to have with the steak. Because of the extra pills I had only had a couple of glasses of wine.

He must have crept in, sneaked upstairs and packed the whole time I was in the kitchen. I turned round and his case was there at the door, his raincoat folded on top.

'Kay, oh God, there's no easy way to tell you this.' He stood next to the suitcase. I thought, I've washed my hair and I've bought steak for dinner. He's wearing a new shirt.

'Kay, come and sit at the table.' But we both stayed where we were.

'Kay, I know you're unhappy, and I have tried to help you -'

I tipped some oil into the frying pan.

'Kay, I'm moving out, I'm going, it's no good anymore. I love you but, honest to God, we're not making each other happy.'

The pills were smudging my thoughts. I took some words and sorted the order in my head before speaking.

'Who is she?'

'She has nothing to do with us.' But he backed towards the suitcase as he said this, and the banging noise started in the room, in my head, a tin plate rattling in each ear. I was squeezing the soft bulb of a mushroom in my hand.

'I'll phone you and we'll sort things out.'

The mushroom was throbbing in my palm. My other hand was holding the knife. The banging had become slashes of noise and I was moving the knife with those slashes, they ran between his body and mine. And then, another layer of noise as the screaming began.

When it stopped, his body folded over the raincoat, on the suitcase.

Love at the Villa Campestri

I read about this writer – I'll call her Helen – who broke up with her lover at a café in Florence. She felt so good that she bought herself an apartment, there, in Florence. She now commutes between her children in the family home in London (she is divorced), and her writing desk in the Florentine apartment.

My husband and I like Italian restaurants: it's where we go to eat when he's not working late. And when we do go out, just the two of us, I pretend I'm on my own. Helen dresses up and eats out alone in Florence. She orders peperoni sott'olio and she chats with the locals. But I have this trick of closing one eye and cutting the table in half between me and my husband. Back and forth, like a pizza cutter, wheeling through the silence between us.

I have imagined that final scene between Helen and her lover, at that café just off the Piazza Santa Croce. The zinc chair legs scratched the cobbles as he stood up; he slapped down a handful of Euros, slopping the espressos in the little white cups. Helen looked at the handbags in the shop window opposite as he walked off. She wiped up the spill of coffee with the paper napkins, kept wiping till the black stain had gone from in front of her. She put the napkins and her departed lover's coffee cup on the waiter's tray. Then she smiled at the waiter and ordered a cappuccino.

Helen crossed the piazza and walked the four sides of the square, one smart shoe just in front of the other, like a child balancing on a wall. It was winter, the square was wide and empty, her idea had the space to spread around her. She was moving on, she loved Florence: she was going to stay there.

I know how Helen felt about that beautiful, magical Italian city. I, too, have walked past the white marble façade of the church of Santa Croce. I have eaten red and yellow peppers, glossy with olive oil. And I fell in love for the first time, for the only time, in Florence.

I was going to Florence to visit Karen and Gemma, university friends who were studying in the city as part of an exchange programme. It was June and I had just finished my first year exams. I travelled to Florence by train, arriving at about seven o'clock in the evening, stepping straight out into the glare of the sunshine and the red and yellow shirts of shouting, laughing Italians. A long train journey away from an exhausted, end of term campus where pale, hungover students sat about listlessly on patches of brown grass.

I bought some cheap sunglasses at a kiosk outside the station, and set off. This was how summer should be. This was the aroma of fresh basil leaves, not the flattened smell of dried herbs in a glass jar. I bought a can of Coke, said 'per favore' and 'grazie' and flirted with the shopkeeper. I never flirted at home. I had my friends' address, I asked, 'Dove -?' and pointed at the scrap of paper. Karen and Gemma's rented apartment was at the top of a dark building in one of the cool, shadowed streets. There was a note pinned to the door. 'Hi Sally, Benvenuto a Firenze! We've gone to a party, see you there!' They gave the address. The front door key was on top of the doorframe. Within half an hour I had dropped my rucksack, washed my face and changed my jeans. I wasn't going to the party, I didn't want my friends to crowd out my impressions of this wonderful place, I wanted to discover it on my own.

I chose a bar behind the Piazzale Michelangelo and ordered a glass of Prosecco. In England I had never been into a pub on my own. I had my Florence guidebook to read, sitting at the bar. But instead, through the mirror behind the bottles of Dubonnet and Cinzano, I watched a group of young Italian men. They all looked the same: handsome, animated faces, gesturing with their Marlboro Lights. But it was Ricardo who stepped forward, like a dancer from the chorus line, like the dance scene in 'West Side Story' when the background blurs behind the two figures. He squeezed a gap at the bar next to me and ordered two Peronis. He handed one to me, we chinked together the green glass bottles. His eyes were dark and shiny, like black olives.

I remember the heat of the bar, and his brown, bony fingers, touching my arm when pausing for the right word in English. I didn't know men's hands could be elegant. My last boyfriend at university, Colin, was a prop forward with hands like oven mitts. Ricardo's English was very good; he was studying medicine at the same university as my friends on their exchange year. He knew some English girls but not Karen and Gemma. I was glad he hadn't met them – especially Karen, with her big eyes and blonde curls.

The warm, night air was heavy with diesel fumes, coffee, and a sweet smell like toasted almonds. Ricardo walked me to my friends' apartment and shook my hand. He shook my hand! I raced up the stairs and opened one of the attic windows onto the street. That sweet smell in the warm air lingered, I wanted to scoop up the whole evening like a huge armful of dark chocolate truffles.

I was asleep when Karen and Gemma returned, and I was up before them the following morning. Ricardo was picking me up on his scooter. I rode behind him, smelt the cigarette smell in his hair, pressed my fingertips against his skinny body, his ribs, like playing notes on a clarinet. We drove out of Florence and along the Mugello valley. I couldn't believe the sunshine, the blue, green and purple landscape, this beautiful Italian boy and his scooter.

'Here we are, Sally. Villa Campestri.'

Ricardo had hinted that his family was well off – the house was stunning. A four-storey building of cream coloured stone and rows of windows covered by bright green shutters. White stone steps led up to double doors of wood and glass. We had driven up a narrow dusty road; the villa stood on its own, its pale face proud and silent in the sun, eyes closed to the valley below.

Ricardo grabbed my hand and we ran up the stone steps. We ran from room to room, dark and cool behind the shutters. We ran up the stairs and into a bedroom. Ricardo pulled back the white sheets and gold embroidered silk bedspread. His skin was the colour of clear honey, he traced the sprinkle of freckles on my white body with his lips.

It was late afternoon when Ricardo pulled back the shutters

and went downstairs. He returned with champagne, bread rolls and peaches. He said it was vintage champagne, very expensive. It could have been Babycham for all I knew, or cared. Breadcrumbs fell on his chest like icing sugar on a cake. He licked the peach juice from around my mouth.

Ricardo was longer the next time he left the room. It was dark outside. After about half an hour I got up, and was walking down the stairs just as the front door opened, and a tall Italian man, his wife and two children, came into the hall. My new found confidence in my pale, freckled, naked body disappeared. I ran back upstairs for a sheet as a loud Italian baritone bellowed, 'Ricardo!'

It was not Ricardo's house, it was his uncle's. Ricardo had been house-sitting for his rich uncle and family. He often did this – the house-sitting and the entertaining of guests. Ricardo lived with his father, mother, grandmother and three sisters, in a four-roomed apartment in Florence.

We drove back on his scooter; I didn't slap his face and he didn't offer a handshake. For the rest of the week, Karen and Gemma showed me Florence: the Uffizi, the Ponte Vecchio, the markets at San Lorenzo. I saw Ricardos everywhere, the smooth skin and those handfuls of black curls that had spread on the white pillows like soft, black petals. Back at university I went out with some more rugby players. I felt smug: I knew what falling in love really was.

That is how the feeling should have stayed, caught in that one day, warm in the palm of a brown, elegant hand. But Ricardo finished his medical training at university in London. The same university as Karen's, Gemma's and mine. We met up again; we graduated and we got together again. I saw the Villa Campestri once more on our honeymoon – but even then, it wasn't the same. We had espressos in the Piazza Santa Croce, just like Helen.

I have not been back to Florence for a long time. I like our house in London, even when Ric is working late, or attending medical conferences abroad. He is in Sweden at the moment, with his colleague Fiona, who has the same blonde hair as my old friend Karen. So I'm not going to buy an apartment like Helen and slip in and out of two different lives. But I shall read her book, the one she is writing in Florence. And I might just write about Ricardo and me in Florence – just that first evening, and the following day. And leave the story there.

My Heart In Exile

Imagine you're separated from your closest friend. And over the years you picture them growing up, growing older without you. But you know them so well, you can adapt the image like a series of police photofits. So: the hair is worn shorter like this, this colour would suit them now, the hands are still delicate and strong; perhaps they wear glasses now for reading. But the bright eyes and the turn of the head remain the same.

And then you get to meet them again. And they – she – is just the person your memory and imagination have pieced together. You would think you'd be gratified by this, but you're not. You think instead how close you must have been to get it so right - but you have not been with them while it happened.

I have just seen Anna again. My childhood friend, companion, sweetheart, sister, girlfriend. My Anna. The girl who learnt to read sitting in the same armchair as me, is now an esteemed academic at Harvard. She is the product of a life we didn't lead together, but that was the life I wanted. And now I cannot return to the rest of my life because it is the one I had to live instead.

Anna and I were children together in post-war Cracow, born out of our parents' survival. We inherited their zest for life, their recklessness and disrespect for everything in authority. But we didn't have to use these traits in order to survive. They were gifts which enhanced our childhood, as we ran together through the city streets, with our friends. I see us all like a butterfly, Anna and me, Anna and Mikel, the antennae at the centre, the other kids fanned out into wings on either side.

I was wild back then with unruly hair and a need to disagree with people. I couldn't sit still, felt stifled by the endless visitors and grown-up conversations in our apartment. The thick smell of soup cooking was another layer of heaviness in the small rooms. Anna sat still, she had - has - this quiet grace, which created a stillness around her. She would read for hours. But for all her seriousness, I could make her laugh – that wonderful laugh throbs now in my memory.

We were allowed to play on our own in my parents' apartment. We ate rye bread and bitter chocolate, and made up games ending in the two of us rolling on the floor together. These weren't such innocent games, either. We pulled apart when we finished our play and smoothed our clothes, sitting on opposite sides of the room, staring wide-eyed at each other. My feelings for Anna were like our tangled limbs: I wanted to tease her, I wanted to look after her, I wanted to keep my arms around her. The taste of bitter chocolate brings back the urgency of those adolescent feelings.

Anna must have been about eleven when I knew I should tell her that I loved her. I waited for her to come, flattening my hair with water and unsteady hands. We had seen an American movie with our friends, and I wished I looked like Robert Mitchum. Anna arrived, breathless from running, her curls jangled by the wind. I took one of her hands without speaking, and led her through to the back room. My mother and grandmother were stirring pots in the kitchen, I didn't want Anna waylaid by their chatter so I kept pulling her on. Anna remained silent, nodded to them, so trusting in her plain navy dress.

I let her hand fall and turned to face her. The pause before a dance, before the music plays. Then I looked at Anna, her patient eyes were waiting.

'Anna, I love you because there is no other woman like you.'

Anna stood still, hands clasped in front of her, holding my eyes with hers; she nodded gravely. Then she lowered her eyelashes and smiled – the heroine in the Mitchum movie – and yanked at the tie I had worn for the occasion, shouting, 'Come on then!' We were into one of our games again.

I'm glad I said it, that those words belonged there for a moment, between us.

Anna and I learnt to play the piano together. I was quicker to learn a piece of music, and would be back outside with our friends whilst Anna continued to practise. My fingers could translate a tune from the music to the keys, but with Anna the clarity of her soul accompanied her playing, like the beat of the soft pedal. I would turn at the door and see her nodding to the music, in time with the dark heads on the crotchets and quavers before her. I knew that Anna should always be a pianist, and maybe if we had stayed together, this would have been so.

It was the autumn of 1958 when we were separated. The year before, the ban on emigration for Polish Jews had been lifted. Our families chose different places of exile, Anna's father having friends in America. My family was always going to Israel. We left first and, on that last day together, Anna's family came to our apartment, dressed in their best clothes for the formality of our farewells. Our mothers had gossiped and argued and embraced in their aprons whilst boiling laundry at the stove, or peeling vegetables on the balcony. Now they stood in unfamiliar hats and newly pressed collars, already held apart by the distance about to expand between them.

I wanted our parents to see Anna and me not as children anymore. I whispered to Anna, 'Can I kiss you in front of them?' We giggled a bit and looked anything but grown up when I reached down towards Anna's face and missed her lips completely. And that was our goodbye, a fumbled attempt to carry our childhood friendship into adulthood.

That was seventeen years ago. Through our families we have tracked each other's lives, with the landmarks of our university degrees, our jobs and our marriages. Just a few days ago, I arrived in New York on business and I called the number that my mother had given me. Anna's voice loosened the drawstring that had strangled my soul for so long. I was speaking to my Anna. She agreed to come from Boston later that day and we arranged to meet in Times Square. I was early and couldn't stand still; I walked the streets in the city's grey sunlight. Was I imagining some Hollywood style reunion? I don't think so, more some punctuation to end the sentence left on a colon seventeen years before. I hunched my shoulders, protecting my exposed heart from the elbows of New Yorkers going home from work.

Oh, but I could have come earlier, I could have inserted this clause into our lives much earlier. I had even booked the plane ticket, and that was long before I had the excuse of business in New York. The children were still small but, even then, my wife and I had withdrawn into our own dark corners, meeting only beneath the chandelier that lit our lives as parents. I stayed late at work until past everyone's bedtime. My mother's letters sent family gossip and small bits of new about Anna, and that morning I had received her letter describing Anna's decision to give up her music.

'Her mother is so upset. She wails on the phone, "She's not my Anna anymore, how can she do this? All that practising, Mikel, all those lessons, gone to waste. And she's talented, everyone says so."'

I had taken the letter and set it down on the top of our piano. I seldom played, and my wife Eva wasn't musical. She was dressing the children upstairs. I put my hands on the keys, I played the chords of Anna's and my early lessons. I could not extract Anna at the piano from my memories of her: it strung them together, the melody that connected my life with hers. It was the musical theme to our shared childhood language. Could I do something? I was used to feeling helpless, an angry, restless helplessness at most things around me. I drove into town and, before going to work, bought a ticket to New York for the following week. But as soon as I was back in the car seat, I knew I wouldn't go. How did I know what Anna felt about me? About anything? I could have sworn she would make music her career, and I had got that wrong.

The ticket stayed in the glove compartment of the car. It can't have been much later that I left home and joined the Israeli army.

But here I was now in New York. And here was Anna, looking just as I knew she would. Small and serious but with an open smile, in a white blouse and navy skirt. I wanted to kiss her, hold her face between my hands, shout out in Polish, but we just stood apart, looking. Anna pointed to a restaurant down the street and we walked there, side by side. Once inside, we were shown to a table by the window. The waiter came and went. I lit a cigarette and looked outside: up to the sky, a blue kite with ribbons of sunlight dangling between the buildings, settling on the yellow taxis, the men in smart suits, the women in bright, belted dresses. So much ordered brightness. Across the table I felt crumpled and overgrown against Anna's smooth surfaces.

'You're an American now, Anna. As sleek as a cat.'

She laughed and touched her hair, her eyebrows; removed the glasses she had worn to read the menu.

'They got their hands on me as soon we arrived. I was plucked like a chicken. But look at you, Mikel, you're just the same. You have your father's height but your mother's face, I think. And you could never sit still.'

We began by feeding each other small, digestible helpings of our lives between Cracow and now. And then we were back in my parents' apartment, reminiscing, like grandparents discussing their favourite grandchildren. These memories worked, her eyes could see inside me and she already knew my heart. There she found verses of poetry I had forgotten I knew. We ordered vodka and I recited the poetry, and then I was talking, talking, our shared language. Not just the Polish words but the sentences threading together our childhood.

Later that week, I met Anna's family again. They were visiting Cambridge for her doctoral ceremony. I was greeted like the prodigal son. And then there was the party, a gathering of all Anna's family and friends from America, in Anna's light, stylish living room. I was so proud of my Anna, surrounded by these clever, articulate people as they honoured her. Her husband was one of these people. I leaned against the wall and watched, waiting to have her to myself again.

And we did have some time together, driving out of Boston, the trees and fields reminding me so much of Poland. We ate bread and apples, we drank bottles of beer and we joked with each other. 'Gimme a break,' she said, and we were off, remembering slang from our childhood. If we were like children again, laughing, running down a hill, the brake of adulthood stopped us just short of the bottom. Once she wiped peach juice from my chin with her finger, and another day I laid my head in her lap whilst she read aloud to me. In the depth of the blue sky above, through the space between the leaves, I had never felt such peace.

'I heard you went out with a cowboy,' I teased.

'Oh yes, a good-looking guy – and wealthy, too. But the strong, silent type – no good for me.'

I talked a little about the children, my estrangement from Eva but, even to me, they did not sound like real people. They did not belong with me at this time. I did not mention my suicide attempt. We talked of Poland now, about being Jewish; I described life in the Israeli army, telling her more than I had told anyone else. We sat over our picnics then we raced over the fields, both wanting to win.

Such wonderful days could not be stretched into the future. I had thrown a stone into the pond of our chosen lives, stirring up the water before it closed over the sunken stone.

We have just said goodbye, here at the airport in New York. We embraced at last. I stood with my hand on my heart - the gesture of our parents - before turning to leave. I have never known such sadness. I will return to Israel, but I don't think we will write to each other. These last few days together were just a step taken into each other's lives, one footprint at the door that was never going to become a series of footsteps invited down the hall. Our time for that was seventeen years ago, when I missed her lips and we started out on our separate lives. Anna and I have reached our full stop.

The Unexpected Guest

Sylvia thought all her guests had arrived, until the doorbell rang. Boxing Day Open House at Sylvia Jolly's is simmering nicely in the living room, a Christmas casserole of leftover neighbours and relatives. The bell rings again and she calls out, 'Can someone get that?' But she is already out of the kitchen, wiping her hands down her pale marzipan jumper. Hands that are dry as baked potatoes in the summer, now red and boiling from the washing up bowl. They have run out of glasses.

Sylvia scrunches her washed in, washed out yellow hair, before opening the door. The hall glows behind her, fringed with gold tinsel on the banister rail and hall mirror. She sees a skinny teenage boy in a woollen hat and dark sweatshirt, holding a fraying holdall.

'Hello?' The question mark hooks onto the clouds of frosty air. The boy is tall and still as the lamp post behind him. He says nothing.

'I know – you're Andrea's friend. Sorry, I've forgotten your name.' They both wait a few seconds. His eyes behind glasses are muddy strands in a frozen pond. Inside the house, voices and music are breathed into the hall then out again, as the living room door opens and closes.

'Sorry love, come in, come in.' Sylvia stands back; the boy wipes his feet on the bit of carpet at the door. Then Sylvia is there with a glass of beer. She opens the door into the living room and nudges him in on the wake of the noise.

'Andrea, look who's here.' The throw in from the touchline made, Sylvia returns to washing glasses and sieving icing sugar over the mince pies.

The boy has fallen at the feet of two small children whose fists punch the insides of crisp bags. He looks up into someone's mouth.

The room is red and salivating with the heat of overfed bodies. Conversation is wreathed in crumbs and spit. The Christmas tree is a spiky set of traffic lights, flicking colours into the heavy, mixed spice air which burns from Sylvia's yuletime scented candle on the piano. Christmas cards, shiny red baubles and faces hang round the room against sky red wallpaper. Another layer of clothing for winter. The television screen in the corner has shaded everyone's faces in cartoon colours, its music is a bass line to the raised treble voices.

'Merry Christmas! Welcome to Sylvia's party!' The boy sees an elderly man, tangerine paper hat over creased foil silver hair. And a dog collar. The vicar's old hands are stumps of ginger root around his glass of whiskey. 'Come and sit over here!' He points to the piano stool. The boy's trainers crush crisps and cracker wrappings. He sits on the stool and sips at his drink, the holdall in his lap. Between the rim of his glass and the turn up of his hat, he looks at the other people in the room.

Two women are leaning together on the sofa. A big and a thin one, a roast potato and a cheese straw baked together. Janet Hardcastle lives next door, a lively woman in her fifties with a chest like a bolster, her arms plumped-up cushions. The same yellow hair as Sylvia, they have their roots done together. Sausage roll pastry clings to Janet's chest like tree bark.

'And another friend wrote in her Christmas card: "Apart from the one setback, I've had a good year." What does she mean – she's had a heart attack or her chiropodist's retired? I don't know if to ring.'

Janet's companion is Auntie Liz, Sylvia's niece. (Uncle Ted is watching Tottenham.) Liz is as thin and sharp as a fruit knife. She irons shirts at the drycleaner's, has five children aged eight years and under. Childminds four more. Auntie Liz lives on sandwich crusts and yoghurts past their sell-by date. She speaks in small bites.

'Dom and Lou, stop it.' The two small children covered in crisp scabs are hers. 'Jinx, turn it down.' This to the denim limbs in front of the TV.

Janet's husband is in hospital following a stroke: she has an overflow of conversation from Christmas Day spent alone. 'And do you get those awful typed letters inside Christmas cards? You know: "This year we crossed Canada on a sledge, had Cherie Blair round for tea and Stanley, who's twelve, is running for Prime Minister."'

The boy has drunk his beer but still holds the bag. The room is a tank of warm air, it soaks the wool of his hat, it presses on the lid of the ceiling. Steam curls the corners of Christmas cards and red balloons sag.

'Top up for anyone?' The vicar's knees click locked as he stands, the paper hat slips on one purple ear like a bacon slicer. The boy now sees another man, sitting low on a cushion. Dark, rainy hair over a copy of the Radio Times. Sylvia's son Gary lives three doors down and delivers pizzas on his motorbike.

'Nothing on, wish Mum had Sky. Have you got Sky?' He smiles shyly at the boy. Little broken teeth softened by Sylvia's puddings, ground down remembering street numbers and extra anchovies. The boy does not answer, Gary's nervous voice continues to dip and rise. A swing in an empty playground.

'I got this book of trivia for Christmas. More people are killed by donkeys every year than plane crashes. There's a loo roll in Scandinavia called Krapp –'

The vicar returns, blocking Gary from view. The swing's seat flies up on its chains and is quiet.

'Don't I know you from somewhere?' The head turns in the dog collar towards the boy. 'The weekly paper maybe? "Local boy defends pensioner against rabid dog" – that sort of thing?' The boy leans down and puts the holdall under the piano stool. Then looks at the vicar. The dark ice in his eyes has broken up in the glare of the room's heat.

'I'm sorry, I'm thinking of someone else.' The vicar's elderly head and neck twist back, a screwcap tightening on a bottle. 'You do look familiar,' is addressed to the door. The vicar knows he lacks something with people. Sharp sermons paraded in his study become rambles through a bramble of words, from the pulpit. He is a crisp shortbread finger, dunked into a cup of warm tea.

Sylvia is back. 'Lou sweetheart, hand these mince pies round, would you? Everyone all right? I'm sorry, love, I didn't realise Andrea's not in here. She must be upstairs with Josie – go on up if you want.' She hands a jar of olives to Janet. 'Open this, Jan?' The lid is off in one twist. Janet's forearm bulges, an aubergine in the new purple sweater. Sylvia pours more lager for the boy from a can, then leans on the sofa arm next to Lizzie.

'Poor lad, he doesn't want to sit with us oldies.' Janet reaches out and touches the boy's sleeve. 'Get anything nice for Christmas, did you luvvie?'

The hot, damp wool of the boy's hat is a creeping trellis on his spectacle frames. Sacks of sweat are stacking up against the sides of his nose, the rims of his glasses. Two spots on his chin run yellow wax. He puts his glass on the piano keys. The notes A flat and B flat tilt into the room as the boy stands. Faces, baubles, plates spin round to look. Jinx's finger on the remote control presses silence from the TV. The boy raises black-sleeved arms in a V shape and he circles round, arms slicing portions of pie in the air. He stamps his feet and shakes his head, humming the echo of a guitar string. The room is still rotating as he slows down, he is the ball on a roulette wheel, and he waits for the wheel to stop before sitting again. The boy removes his hat; his hair is as black and sodden as the wool. He pulls up the holdall from between the piano stool legs, and stuffs in the hat.

Jinx nods to himself: the performance is over, he coats the room again with TV sound. Sylvia gets up to turn on lights and draw curtains. The street lamp, an orange boiled sweet, well sucked, glows through a gap in the curtains. Sylvia finds chocolates for the children, strokes Gary's head, collects empty plates – strings the party back together.

'You all right there, Lizzie? Ted coming later?'

'Doubt it.' Her words clip like clothes pegs onto her aunt's sympathy.

'Lovely party, Sylvia – as always!' Sylvia takes the vicar's empty whiskey glass.

No one hears the doorbell, but the broad thumps boom against the walls. Sylvia goes out again. The men's voices stay on the doorstep, the front door open. A sheet of ice slips under the living room door. Through the gap in the curtains a blue light flares, a cold spray on the red walls and red faces. Dom and Lou climb over their mother on the sofa and look out.

'It's a police car.'

'Mummy, there's a police car, why –'

'Police? God knows. Get down –'

'Knowing Mum, she'll ask them in.' They all look at Gary: the vicar, Janet and Liz, Jinx, Dom and Lou. The boy on the piano stool scrapes his chin, wipes the inside of his glass with a finger, then licks it.

Sylvia returns. The blue heart stops beating in the room.

'Sorry about that, two policemen – nice, they were. One of them went to your school, Gary.'

'So what did they want?' Her son asks.

'Just making door-to-door enquiries, they said. Had we seen anything. Burglars love Christmas - houses chocka with presents.'

'All those new DVD players and Xboxes.' Gary looks wistful.

'I hope I locked my door,' Janet says. 'I'd hate someone to touch my bits and pieces.' Her elbow nudges Liz as she grins, a soft roll against a breadstick.

'It's young lads doing it, they said. But they're not sure how - there's no breaking in or anything.'

'Down the chimney, maybe. Ho ho ho.'

'So you believe in Father Christmas?' Jinx asks the vicar.

'Well, I, -'

'He looks a bit like God, with the beard and everything? But God doesn't have reindeer, does he - '

'Shut up, Jinx.' Liz frowns at her oldest son. 'Watch the telly.'

'Anyway, I did ask them, but they didn't have time for a drink.'

'Thank God for that.' Janet, Liz and Gary together.

Sylvia's information hovers in the room, a lazy seabird debating a dive.

'Now, what about some music?' Sylvia pulls the thread on the party again. 'You'll play, won't you Janet? Jinx, turn the telly down a bit?'

'And would you mind, love?' Sylvia touches the arm of the boy on the piano stool. He stands up, everyone is watching him. Sylvia's earlier words are still hanging on the horizon.

'Hey, let's have some port whilst Janet plays.' Sylvia leaves the room and this time the boy follows her. She stops in the hall as he puts his hat on.

'Are you going, sweetheart? I'm sorry about Andrea, I should have gone up.' She tugs the sleeves of various jackets and raincoats on the hall coatstand.

'Is this yours?' She pulls down a leather jacket and they look at each other. Sylvia's gentle blue eyes. The dark, jagged cracks in the boy's eyes have gone. He shakes his head, opens the front door and turns on the doorstep.

'Thank you for the party.'

'Pleasure. Hey, come here,' and she hugs him, feels a thinly wrapped parcel. 'Happy New Year, love. Will you be all right? Call in again, won't you?'

Looking for her Story

The shop was quiet that morning, umbrellas heading straight for the tearooms. No one wanted to look at local prints and pottery, in dripping clothes. Cold, red fingers wanted to hold hot chocolate mugs and cups of tea.

Beth sat by the till with her notebook. An ideal quiet time for some writing. John had caught the early train to London for one of his visits to the art galleries; they both looked forward to these days on their own.

Beth and John were well known local artists, John for his watercolours of Bakewell town centre, the River Wye's bridge and the low, wet fields. Tourists to the Peak District admired the pale washed watercolours in slate grey tones, lavenders and sage greens. A surprising detail in a windowsill edged in black ink, or a sunlit pub sign. They illustrated the artist himself, Beth had always thought, her pale, languid husband with his brittle light brown hair and beige corduroy trousers. But eyes the colour of brown ale, behind the wire glasses. And those lean fingers holding the paint brush, fingers that Beth had found attractive and sensual when they first knew each other, some twenty years ago.

And Beth herself, she wrote stories. They were published in pamphlet form with the poetry and prose of other aspiring local writers, and were sold in the town's bookshops. Local tales of small town life, the bolts securing the lives of local farmers and townspeople: their lives and conversations inlaid on the blurred grey landscape. Beth saw herself apart from this rural community, and knew that the lack of depth and creativity in her own life meant she was unable to give any depth of expression to the lives of her characters.

'I would have found it with Shell,' she told herself. Together she and Shell would have dug up the colour and meaning of life from the wide flowing river and the flat fields surrounding them.

And how did customers coming into the shop see Beth? A slight figure with neat ash brown hair, sitting by the till in a powder blue or lemon John Lewis cardigan, a gold necklace or amber beads matching a bright but cautious gaze. If they looked below the counter there were rather expensive shoes.

Beth would have liked to identify herself with the vividly painted crockery and candle holders they sold, commissioned from students at the local art college. The abstract tangerine cat motifs on teapots; swirls of lime and turquoise wrapped round jugs and espresso cup handles. Beth knew such colours were within her but nothing urged them to her fingertips, to splash out on the blank, white page. Scratchy words replaced such bold, colourful strokes. Her quiet life produced quiet stories, rejected by the London publishers she had approached one unusually bright morning. The 'manuscript assessment' she had sought on a literary website confirmed what she knew. 'Tidy stories but with limited appeal. Characters rather flat, no depth of feeling.'

The door opened and a biker came in, carrying his helmet, rain dripping from the fringing on his black leather.

'It's pissing it down out there,' he said, putting his helmet on a low display shelf of tie and dye scarves.

Beth smiled and looked down.

'You don't have a caff back there, do you?' he asked, pointing at the gallery at the back of the shop.

'I'm afraid not.'

He walked passed Beth at the till, blank notebook on her lap. She smelt his damp leather and cigarettes.

'You could do, you know. Have a teashop here. Instead of–' and he waved his arm at John's watercolours on display. Rain flicked off the fringing on his arm, splashing a picture of the church.

'You know, a few scones, homemade coffee cake – you could make your own. Oh hang on, these aren't *your* pictures, are they?'

'As a matter of fact, they're not. They're –' Beth hesitated.

He came back into the front of the shop.

'Good, I was hoping they weren't. Think about the scones, though.' He grinned, cheekily rather than mockingly, and picked up his helmet.

'I'd better find my cappuccino elsewhere then,' and he grinned again. 'You look as if you could do with a bit of warming up as well.'

Beth tried to give a little laugh.

'See you then. Good luck with those pictures.'

Beth fetched a cloth and wiped where the motorbike helmet had wet the glass display. She felt hot with embarrassment, disloyalty to John and an attraction to the outspoken, attractive young man. She remembered her laugh as he left.

'God, I sounded like a stuck up doorbell.'

A family came into the shop, waterproofs and ice-lolly juice spilling: they bought a few postcards. Beth wiped up after them. Back at the till she thought how Shell would have had a boyfriend now like that biker. She saw them laughing as they left the shop, then sitting with their cappuccinos, a striped woollen hat over Shell's long fair hair.

'Oh Mum's alright really, doesn't get out often enough. Christmas shopping in Leeds and the odd trip to the Royal Exchange is as exciting as it gets.'

A friend in Beth's book group came in for some candles, and they talked a bit about their current book by Zadie Smith. Beth returned to her notebook. She was trying a new story using one of her regular characters, a flighty farmer's daughter who had turned down the village schoolteacher. Beth felt that Caitlin had promise and could have a story of her own, if she left the bland backdrop of the town. An attempt at a bold flourish. Beth thought of the struggle Zadie Smith might have encountered to find such characters in Bakewell.

She thought of John in London. He had set off that morning following his daily routine of a cup of tea for Beth in bed, a boiled egg and Radio 4 for himself at the breakfast bar, then a kiss blown through the bedroom door.

'Bye, love. Hope the shop's not too busy. Planning some writing?'

Beth and John had met at Nottingham University, holding their wedding the week after the degree ceremony. They had both wanted children and eagerly started an active sex life, whilst newly-married postgraduate students, on damp weekends in the Lake District. Beth could still see the clammy inside of their tent, and feel her muffling nylon sleeping bag zipped up to John's. But, beyond those artistic fingers carefully undoing shirt buttons, the details of their bodies together eluded her. In the first year of their marriage, on a chilling January evening, they had grasped each other on their way home from the pub. Glowing from the fire at the Red Lion and the steaming steak and kidney pie, they had laid down in a field. Beth had been sure such a sudden act of passion would produce a child, but it remained just John and herself in their one-bedroomed flat in Nottingham.

Then it happened. Still in their one-bedroomed flat, John having grown a beard and started evening art classes, Beth writing reviews for amateur dramatic productions in the evening newspaper, and a little bit of poetry. Beth became pregnant, didn't remember the night she conceived, but spent nine months feeling warm, soporific, waiting.

Shell was stillborn at nine months. They had chosen Catherine as a girl's name, but this baby was Shell to Beth. A baby in a smooth, warm shell, who decided not to uncurl for the world and for Beth.

So Beth never knew if motherhood could have tapped into the rich layer of language she knew flowed within her. She and John saw the shop for sale in Bakewell, and thought about a new start. Beth whitewashed the walls, constructed the glass display cabinets, sought suppliers and attended bookkeeping lessons. John waded across damp fields, bony elbows banging against the easel under his arm. They discovered a favourite French restaurant in the area and ate out once a month. They still shared the same bed but came to it in shifts, Beth retiring early to read, John painting until late. When John completed a watercolour, he might tug drowsily at Beth's nightgown, and Beth would usually roll over towards him.

Shell remained in her pink shell. Over the years Beth thought of what they would have shared as mother and daughter. Learning to write and draw, climbing hills and picking blackberries, making a proper Bakewell Pudding with its rich yellow sweetness. Then more adventurous schemes together, trekking the mountains of Europe and discovering characters to write about on train journeys and in Swiss hotel foyers.

If only Shell had chosen to be part of Beth's life.

Beth turned the sign to 'Closed' at six o'clock, locked up, and took the accounts with her up to their flat above the shop. It maddened her that she was good with figures, imagining the left side of her brain cramping any creativity from the right side. The amount of September rain had affected sales, there was little work to do. She lit a couple of pale yellow lamps in their small sitting room, poured herself a Scotch and ginger and eased her shoes off with her toes.

The telephone rang.

'Hello?'

'Is this Beth?'

'Who is this?'

'My name's Jackie – you don't know who I am?'

'No.'

'Oh God, I should wait for John to come back.'

'John?' Beth sat forward on the sofa. 'John's there – are you in London?'

'God no –'

'Where's John – I don't understand.'

'If you must know, he's just stormed out.'

John *stormed* out?

'I think there's some sort of mistake. Are we talking about John Foster? From Bakewell? My husband John?'

'That's him alright, your husband. Well, I told him I was going to make this call, and so – John and I have been seeing each other, having an affair, for the last eight years.'

' Beth hung on in silence for a minute, asked for the woman's number and put the phone down. She felt a strange, warm, swelling inside her, throwing up words and an unfamiliar feeling of release. She grabbed the accounts book beside her and was scribbling them down, a poem: she had not written poetry for years. John ... an affair all these years. Beth felt no anger, it was almost excitement, she saw him with this Jackie, imagined a dark haired young woman in mini skirt and boots.

Beth phoned the number back and Jackie answered.

'He's not come back yet.'

'I'm coming over now, let me have your address.'

'What now?'

'Yes, now, I want to see you both,' and again Beth felt this surge of excitement. She thought of other people in this woman Jackie's life, a whole cast spreading out from the central character.

Beth took the address in Leeds and some directions. She rushed around the flat, tidying up then going into the bedroom to change her skirt and shoes.The lines of poetry lit up every movement. She hadn't eaten any supper so took an apple from the fruit bowl on the breakfast bar. Beth saw John eating his boiled egg there that morning and she laughed hysterically. Her doorbell tinkle had disappeared.

Beth walked down and through the shop, then returned upstairs for her notebook. She found pencils in the top drawer of the bureau, sharpened them to points, ran her fingers smoothly down their lengths. In the hall, she pulled down a yellow and cherry red silk scarf, never worn. This she wrapped round her neck in front of the mirror. Her eyes were sharp blue sparks watching.

Beth locked the shop door behind her. She walked along the wet street in the darkening September evening, her fiery scarf flowing. She had found her story.

The Affair

Helen had decided she would tell her husband tonight that she was going to have an affair. She chose the candlelit dinner approach, quite prepared to spend time in both the kitchen and the bedroom to get her own way. She had spent the last half an hour marinating peppers, changing her underwear and pushing children's toys into cupboards.

Andrew had called from his mobile on the tube, he would be back soon. The table was set with a cream linen tablecloth, gold candles and three bottles of red wine, co-ordinating with the autumn leaf pattern on the dinner service. The perfect background for the red pesto apricot chicken. Helen had opened the French windows onto their small terraced house garden; it was raining and Helen shivered as the cold air smoothed the skin on her back. She was wearing a black halter-neck top bought that morning. Elvis Costello sang from the CD player, reminiscent of nights snogging on Andrew's bedsit sofa.

Daisy and Harry had obligingly gone to sleep early, having licked out the bowl from the vodka chocolate torte.

Helen had already decanted two of the wine bottles. She poured a glass from the nearest bottle and raised this in the air. 'Here's to you, Vicky, thanks for the inspiration,' she said, recalling their meeting last week.

Vicky had arrived at the Starbucks coffee shop half an hour late, designer shop carrier bags slapping against her high-heeled boots. She looked stunning. Her long red hair had been cropped into a short bob streaked with golds; her thin face glowed under blusher, an excited laugh was framed by plum coloured lips. Vicky used to say she looked in a mirror and saw a red setter: today she was a sleek, rare bird. Helen got up, thinking that her own poodle look of curly hair, bobbly jumpers and short legs remained unchanged. 'My God, Vicky – no, don't say anything, I'll get the coffees and you can tell me everything.'

'Thanks, Helen, can you make mine an espresso?'

Helen returned from the counter. Monday morning, and the coffee shop was busy with women either feeding shortbread to toddlers, or tapping on their laptops.

'OK, what's going on? What's all this new hairdo, clothes, make up, espresso business? Oh – and jewellery.'

Vicky had pushed her sleeves back; a gold bangle the width of Sellotape rolled on her wrist.

'Helen, I'm so happy, I never thought I'd feel like this again. It's like skipping school or stealing sweets or kissing the teacher. Remember Mr Harris?'

Helen had been spooning cappuccino froth into her mouth. She stopped. 'You're not having an affair, are you? Oh my God.'

'You can tell?'

'Well, you don't eat sweets anymore, you have sweeteners. And assuming it's not hunky Harris… who is it?'

'Someone at the gym, he's called Mike. His office is near here but he lives in Surrey.'

'Along with his wife and children, I suppose.'

'No, he's divorced, and – he – is – gorgeous.' Vicky sighed, Helen grunted.

'And what about *your* family, what about Jack?'

Vicky's glossy lips smooched with the espresso cup. Helen felt depressed, and watched the mother at a nearby table trying to remove pureed apple from her hair with a paper napkin. Even this failed to cheer her up.

'Vicky, I'm sorry to sound so Victorian and disapproving, I can't help it, you're being so bloody breathy and girly about it. Once the kids were at school, we were going to go back to work, remember? Not start bonking the first available man in the sauna.'

'It beats being an accountant.' That irritating giggle again.

'If I can tell, don't you think James can?'

'James just thinks I've had my hair cut and bought some new

clothes. Anyway, I'm happier at home, I recite poetry whilst I do the ironing.'

They both looked at each other and laughed.

'Seriously, though, is it just a fling or – I sound like your mother now.'

'I don't know. Oh Helen, it's just so nice to talk – we do talk as well – about things, rather than discussing schools and babysitters and mortgages. We send each other silly text messages. I just feel fancied and spoilt and –'

Helen watched Vicky's face and saw her thoughts leave Starbucks for some hotel room. And she had gone soon afterwards, meeting Mike for the remaining hours before the bell rang at Jack's school. Helen stayed for another coffee before going home in a daze.

For the rest of the week the idea of Vicky and another man followed her round Tesco's, to an interview at a job agency, even into bed with her and Andrew. Then last night she had dreamt she was standing in a bathroom doorway wearing nothing but Vicky's bangle. She had said, 'I've got a message for you,' but it was dark in the room and as she crossed to the bed, she didn't know who she would find there. It was Andrew. The shock woke her and she sat up in bed. From the dark shadows of her dream, the idea came to her.

Two glasses of wine later, Andrew arrived home. Helen met him in the hall and gave him a Beaujolais-flavoured kiss. The rain had flattened his hair, he looked like Clark Kent. She removed his glasses and wiped them on her skirt before putting them back with another kiss.

'Hello, darling.'

'You look nice – very sexy. Are the children in bed already?'

'Oh yes, it's just toi et moi. We're having a candlelit dinner.'

'Great, give me a minute to change.'

As Andrew went upstairs, Helen lit the candles, sliced ciabatta bread and poured Andrew a glass of wine, refilling her now empty one. Rather unsteadily she sat at the table.

Well into the second bottle, and between mouthfuls of wild rice and chicken, Helen introduced the subject.

'Have you ever thought of having an affair, Andrew?'

'Course not, what a question! Why?'

'What about those skinny young things in the marketing department, haven't you charmed them with your big blue eyes?'

'Only when I've got a deadline to meet.'

'OK, do you know many people who are cheating on their other halves?'

'One or two – no, only one I think. What *are* you reading at the moment, Helen?'

'You see, I've got this theory that it's not another person they're after – you know, someone taller, richer, funnier or whatever. It's the situation. You know: lunches, hotel suites, presents, the secrecy of it all. Pillow-talk instead of the-sheets- need-washing talk.'

'I love you, darling, I don't want an affair. Is there more rice?'

Helen fetched the dish from the kitchen.

'I saw – well, it doesn't matter who - this week, and OK, she's seeing someone else.'

'Vicky, by any chance?'

'How do you – I didn't say – anyway, I suppose I was jealous, she was like another woman with all the flirtation and everything. And I couldn't understand why I felt jealous, loving my husband as I do –' Helen took Andrew's free hand - the other was forking rice into his mouth. He had a smear of pesto sauce on his chin, but was a sensitive soul despite his large build – so she didn't tell him.

'So,' she stopped until Andrew looked at her. 'Why don't you - next time we're meeting for lunch – book a hotel room for afterwards?'

Andrew removed his hand to have a gulp of wine. He coughed, gave a short laugh, said, 'I think it's time you went back to work. You're under the influence of too many Cosmopolitan magazines.'

'No, I'm being serious. Think about it. Wouldn't it be fun, no children, no discussions about converting the loft or paving the garden. Just us and room service.'

Andrew had placed his glasses amongst the ciabatta crumbs on his side plate and was rubbing his eyes. Helen stroked his cheek. 'You could send me a text message saying where to meet. Then we could meet the same time every week, same room, and pretend like we were lovers.'

Andrew moved away from Helen's hand; he got up and closed the French windows. It was dark outside, the rain was splintering against the glass. Elvis Costello had put his guitar down a long time ago. Andrew drew the curtains against the night and on their conversation.

'OK, end of subject, I understand.' Helen blew out the candles. The chocolate torte stayed in the fridge. Later, they made love in their bedroom, surrounded by photos of the children and piles of laundry.

She had another go, though, in the morning, coming up behind Andrew whilst he drank his coffee and putting her arms around his waist. She loved him in his City suit, all smart before the crumpling of the day.

'So how about it, lover boy?'

'Not that again, Helen, it's daft, and it's - it's not normal.'

'Where's your sense of adventure, don't you remember doing it in the Rugby Club toilets?'

'Yeah - that was before children and everything else.'

'*But that's just my point*!' Helen poured Ready Brek into two bowls. 'OK, OK, forget it.' She took out the milk carton and slammed the fridge door, thought of her day ahead: drycleaners, making Bolognese sauce, visiting her mother. Irritation curled around her next words to Andrew. 'Can you hurry the kids up?'

Helen telephoned Vicky later that morning and told her about her idea. Vicky's reaction was the same as Andrew's, but she laughed a lot more. They arranged to go to the cinema later that week. To distract herself, Helen filled four binliners to take to the charity shop. The following day Harry was ill, so she spent several hours reading Shirley Hughes, drawing trains and making milkshakes. Over dinner she and Andrew discussed Harry's sore throat and their holiday in Cornwall. Then, that night, she had the naked-at-the-bathroom-door dream again, but this time the bed disappeared and she was standing in the school playground with nothing on. She woke feeling depressed.

Helen had mixed feelings about seeing Vicky, as she knocked on her door on Friday evening. Please don't come out with all that yucky Mike stuff, she thought. After knocking three times, the door was opened by James holding a sleepy Jack on his shoulder.

'Hi James, is Vicky ready?'

'Vicky's out, she's gone to the gym.'

'Oh no, I must have got the wrong evening,' she said, thinking, '*Oh no, I bloody well know where you are.*'

'Why don't you come in? I've just opened a bottle and you'll stop me feeling like a sad old git drinking on my own.'

Helen grinned and followed them in. She didn't know James that well, the four of them had met for dinner a couple of times. He was a quiet man with a soft Scottish accent, and sandy hair that matched his chinos. Not very tall, and certainly smaller than Vicky in her current size heels. He had got very loud the last time they all went out for a curry, telling them stories of his Glaswegian upbringing.

'I'll just put this wee boy to bed. Say night night to Helen.' Helen kissed Jack's warm, flushed cheek then went into the living room. This was a more elegant version of her own, with white sofas, abstract paintings, grown-up novels on the shelves and interior design magazines on the coffee table. Jack had his own playroom off the kitchen. Helen tucked her curly brown hair behind her ears and, looking in the mirror over the fireplace, wished she had put on some lipstick. Everyone told her how young she looked, but she wished they meant twenty-five rather than fifteen.

James came in with a bottle of white wine and two glasses.

'How are you doing, Helen, I haven't seen you for ages. Not since I disgraced myself in the Taj Mahal.'

'The Star of India, actually. We had a good evening.'

'So, what are you up to, now? Vicky says you're looking for another job.'

'A bit half-heartedly, though. I don't want to go back to editorial work, I'm waiting for something to grab me really. Tell me about your job.'

They sat on one of the white sofas, half-watching Brookside with the sound turned down, chatting about James' job as a journalist. Helen thought how relaxed he was, away from Vicky's hyper-personality. James was telling her about a colleague at work whose wife had run off with her personal trainer. Helen felt herself blushing (like a fifteen year old), and, to alter the course of the conversation, told James about her husband and wife affair idea. She presented it as a hypothetical scenario of course. James listened without comment, then said,

'So, he sends her a short, sexy e-mail and they meet in the lunch hour, order oysters and champagne. Same hotel room, but she waits at home – or at her desk if she's working - for his message on the screen. Or even better, they have their own apartment. Perhaps I could get the paper to fund it and I could carry out some research with Vicky?' He looked at Helen. 'Or - do you think Andrew would be up for it?'

Helen ignored the nip of disloyalty; she was still exasperated with her husband.

'All right then, I was thinking about Andrew and me. But he was just embarrassed. We'll probably go away for a weekend instead.'

'No, not the same thing. What if you set it all up, booked a room somewhere and then e-mail him, giving him, say, half an hour's notice?

'He'd probably say he was working through lunch.'

'OK, send a text message to his mobile. More personal: harder to ignore.'

'You mean, just give the time and place and then turn up and wait?'

'Yes, brilliant. Now where would be really good?'

'I've always wanted to stay at that new art deco place behind Piccadilly, it's called by the number of the street.'

I know. Two One Two, they have a decent selection of whiskies.

OK, so, choose the day – Friday would be good, he'll be less in work mode. James picked up a biro and started writing on the cover of 'House and Garden'. 'Right, something like, 'It's all booked, room number whatever, at Two One Two, St James'. Meet me at 12 o'clock in the bar.' No, better still, say: 'Meet me in a hour', more mysterious, more sexy. Shall we open another bottle, I'm really getting into this?'

Helen was giggling. 'Don't you dare write an article on this, remember it's my idea. Thanks for the wine, I'd better not have any more, I only had half a fish finger before coming out.'

'I think you should go for it. Andrew will love it once he's there.' They both got up, James kissed Helen's cheek at the front door, said, 'We must all go out together again soon. Chinese maybe this time?'

Helen was typing up her CV on the computer the next morning. She got bored and sent an e-mail to Andrew at work: 'Any rude jokes circulating round the office?' Then she made herself a cup of coffee and settled down on the Internet, looking at Two One Two's website. She had great fun reading room service menus and descriptions of the different suites.

On Friday morning she took the children to school, returned home and telephoned the hotel. She then had a bath until eleven o'clock when she called Andrew's mobile number and sent the message.

Helen hated bar stools, they rearranged your underwear and were unflattering to legs, especially short ones like hers. But the barman had been friendly, and she needed an ally. The hotel was all white with slashes of silver: silver mirror frames and light fittings, and the long zinc bar. She imagined the designer eating a takeaway curry, removing his naan bread from the paper bag with the foil inside – and finding his inspiration. Helen was wearing her zip-up leather jacket and short black skirt; a spacesuit would have been more suited to the surroundings.

Twelve-thirty came and she ordered a second Smirnoff Ice. She checked again that her mobile was switched on. 'Idiot, idiot,' she chanted under her breath, not sure if she meant herself or Andrew.

'He didn't turn up, did he?' Helen turned from counting the number of optics behind the bar. There stood James. She shook her head.

'Did you book the room and everything?' She didn't bother to nod.

'Can I buy you a drink – or shall we go and check they put the champagne on ice?'

Helen slid slowly off the barstool on the silk of her underskirt. She took out her mobile to switch it off, and followed James who had already called the lift.

Lizzie's Jack

'Wasn't it awful, Lizzie's Jack dying like that.' Liane opens their Thursday night conversation. The four women take their drinks from the bar to their usual table, remove their Tesco overalls and sit down.

'What do you mean, like that?' Janet asks.

'You know – no notice or anything.'

'No notice! He could hardly have given notice, could he? I mean, he wasn't going to put a postcard in the newsagent's window: "I'm expecting to die next Friday; if any of my friends would like to join me in a last drink?"'

'You know what I mean, and he wasn't that old. He must have been about your age, Janet.'

'Well, it just shows you. Carpe Diem and all that.'

'Carpet what?'

'Carpe Diem, stupid. It means make the most of things. It was in that film with Robin Williams.'

'What – Mrs Doubtfire?'

'For God's sake, Liane. No, the one where he's a teacher at a posh school. Something about poets. Anyway, Robin Williams says, "Carpe Diem".'

'Carpie DM. Is it Greek or something?' Liane turns to Julie who has been picking at her nails and drinking her Bacardi and Coke. 'Hey Julie, you've been to Greece, can you speak the language?'

'Nah, don't need to. Kebab means a kebab in any country, dunnit?'

'So anyway.' Janet takes control of the conversation. 'How's Lizzie taking it – Jack dying and all that?'

'I don't really know, she's been off work. I only know as much as you do, from what Mr Storehouse said in that meeting at lunchtime.'

'We ought to go and see her, you know. I mean, she's not my best mate, but we've all had a few drinks together, haven't we?'

Carole now puts down her pint of lager. 'You know Barbara, the one with the Dame Edna glasses? Husband ran off with their neighbour's teenage daughter.' Half way down her pint, Carole usually joins in like this. 'She works on the checkout next to Lizzie and she's been round to the house.'

'And how was she?'

'Well she didn't tell me, I was in the Ladies and she was talking to one of the other girls. But get this: Jack – the body – was still lying on their bed.'

'Oh God, what? No! That means he's been there for - how long?' Liane puts down her bag of bacon crisps.

'Well this was a couple of days ago. But he must have been on the bed since the weekend.'

'That is really gross. Don't they start smelling, I mean –'

'Shut up, Liane.' Janet nods at Carole to continue.

'So Lizzie,' Carole says, 'goes off to sleep in the spare room.'

'Not the first time she's done that. Most Friday nights, from what I've heard.'

'Liane! What's that supposed to mean?'

'You know Jack likes – sorry, liked - a pint or two. Well, on a Friday night, after the bookies and the pub, he'd come home –'

'No, we don't want to know, Liane, you also listen to too many conversations in the bog. Come on girls, who's ready for another?'

Janet goes to the bar and returns with four more drinks. There's a long silence between them – of about ten seconds.

'The thing is.' Julie speaks for the first time since her contribution about Greek cuisine. 'The thing is, Jack was in the bookies only yesterday.'

'Don't be stupid, Jules. He's dead, for God's sake.'

'No, it was him, honest Jan, it was Jack.'

'Where were you? I bet you were in the hairdresser's across the road – and you couldn't see from there.'

'I just know.' The Coke in Julie's drink leaves a tidemark of black round her mouth. 'OK, I know, because I'd just had a sandwich with him in the Greyhound.'

The other three glasses hit the table at the same time: vodka, wine and lager mix in a surprised splash of gold. Janet, Liane and Carole look at Julie.

'Julie – what are you saying?' Janet leans towards her.

But Julie gets up and pulls on her leather jacket. 'I've got to go, just forget it. I'll see you at work tomorrow.' She leaves the pub.

Janet cannot think what to say so she goes to the Ladies. Carole lights a cigarette and Liane checks her phone messages.

Janet returns to the table and waits. Liane can be relied upon to get the conversation going again.

'So Janet,' Liane looks nervously across the table. 'Do you think Lizzie'll be coming for a drink tonight?'

'To be honest, I don't know what to think.'

'Why don't we give her a ring, then we'd know for sure about – about Jack.'

'Oh yeah, right. So we phone her up and say, "Hi Lizzie, we're down the pub, are you coming? Oh, and is it true that your Jack won't be placing any more bets?"'

'You're always so sarcastic, Janet. Couldn't we just phone her and see what she says?'

'Liane's right.' Carole stubs out her cigarette. 'Let's just phone her, she's bound to say something which gives it away.'

Liane and Carole take Janet's lack of response for agreement, and Liane reaches in her handbag for her mobile phone.

'I don't believe it, you can put your phone away, Liane. She's here.' Janet knocks back her vodka and takes a deep breath.

'Hi everyone, sorry I'm late. Same drinks as usual?' Lizzie drops her coat onto the stool vacated by Julie and goes to the bar. The other three can't look at each other, they lower their heads as though about to start a game of Bingo.

Lizzie brings a tray over. 'Still drinking pints, Carole?' They take in her usual made up face, lipstick applied, nicely ironed blouse. No shakes as she sips her Smirnoff Ice.

'What've I missed then, what's the gossip?'

Nervous giggle. This is Liane. 'Oh nothing, the usual, you know.'

'That isn't true.' Janet's large hands grip the table top as she grips hold of the subject. 'Lizzie, you've got to tell us. What's going on with Jack?'

'Jack? What do you mean – what's he got to do with anything?'

'Lizzie, you've been off work on compassionate leave. And Mr Storehouse told us –'

'God, you can't hide much from you lot, can you?' Lizzie opens her bag of dry roasted. 'Jack's gone away for a while, that's all. He's not feeling too good –'

'Not feeling too good? I thought he was out cold –'

'Liane, shut up.' Janet kicks her under the table.

'Anyway, he's going to his Dad's for a bit. He lives in Hastings, got a nice flat overlooking the sea.'

'It's pebbly, the beach there, isn't it?' Janet looks at Liane after this remark but lets her continue. 'We went there once when I was little, but I remember there was no sand. Our B & B smelt of stale milk. Shall I see if Danny will let us do karaoke tonight?'

Mistress of the House

He had started to change about a month ago, not long after they moved in. Maddie thought of the Adam she had met three years before: everyone's friend, buying the next round, organising skiing trips and running marathons for charity. He brought along six friends on their second date. She had wanted to shut a door and have him to herself. Have those green eyes look at her and not the rest of the room.

He had gone to work now. Maddie was alone with the cottage and the cold, grey morning. She had a doctor's appointment that afternoon and had taken the day off to sort out the house.

His behaviour last night still caused her to clatter the breakfast plates and cups. They had been meeting old friends from town, showing off their very own local village pub. Maddie had washed her hair and taken time with her make up: she had got over the early sickness but still looked pale. She tied her long fair hair with a ribbon that matched her new emerald green jumper and walked down the open stairs into the living room. Adam was sat by the fire, reading a book.

'Adam, shouldn't we be going now?'

He didn't look up, said, 'I'd quite like to stay in tonight.'

'What do you mean? We're meeting Joe and Allie in the pub – like, now.'

Adam sat absolutely still, long legs stretched out in front of the fire.

'Have you got a cold or something?'

He looked up at this. He was never ill. 'What?'

'Well, you're so lethargic. Come on, I could do with a night out.'

But, she had telephoned their friends, and they had stayed in. It had worried Maddie, seeing Adam like that: his long arms and legs were never still. But she felt she had seen him sitting there like that before. Then she got mad, made four pints of vegetable soup, and stripped some wallpaper on the stairs. Adam microwaved a lasagne and was asleep when she came to bed.

Maddie put the milk bottles on the doorstep, the glass clinking against the quiet of the lane. It didn't feel like real life, living in the country after their apartment in town. The still air and flat cottages were not filled out by constant voices, cars, movement.

Maddie took a cup of coffee upstairs and into the small back bedroom. This had been a junk room for years, they had added theirs to the boxes already there. She decided it could be a pretty room with the sloping ceiling and view over fields. She planned to paint it in yellows and greens and imagined a cot and a rocking chair in there. She sat on a box of photograph albums; these had belonged to Adam's grandparents. They had inherited the cottage from his grandfather when he died. Adam's father lived in the States and had been happy for Adam to have the place.

'Dad hated this cottage,' Adam had told Maddie, the first time they had looked round. Maddie was feeling excited, looking at the stone floor, the open fire and beamed ceilings.

'But why - it's lovely, a bit shabby maybe.'

'I don't know, he said visiting Gran and Grandpa did his head in. He used to go to the pub after ten minutes.'

'How long did your grandparents live here?'

'About ten years I think. Grandpa in that chair by the fire and Gran rushing about making cups of tea – he just sat there.'

Adam had pointed at the threadbare dark red armchair next to the fireplace. He sat down and rubbed the arms.

'God, it smells the same, of Grandpa in this house. His old jacket, sort of stale and woolly.'

'He must have changed then, he struck me as a bit of a livewire,' Maddie said. She had visited him a couple of times in the old people's home. 'Those fancy ties he wore, all that flirting with the nurses.'

'I know, after Gran died and he moved out of here – he was so different.'

Maddie moved boxes onto the landing. As the room emptied, and some delicate sunlight lifted the faded feeling of the room, Maddie heard a humming sound. She thought it was the washing machine downstairs or the central heating, but it became the hum of a low voice. Maddie looked out of the window over the garden but the voice was in the room. It wasn't frightening, she sat on the faded pink carpet and listened. The hum wasn't strange to her, it had been in the background of the cottage since they moved in. Behind the wallpaper, under the floorboards, it belonged to the house.

She couldn't make out any words, it was a low female voice and it was agitated. Then it stopped. Maddie found the silence more disconcerting, she opened the window. But the sash didn't work and, after trying to force it open, she saw it had been painted shut.

The room was still quiet, but looking over the fields outside, Maddie could feel a movement in the room. It gave her energy, she fetched a scrubbing brush and bucket of water and rolled back the old carpet. It felt good brushing hard at the floorboards. Maybe they could stain the wood and have a sheepskin rug next to the cot. The brush underneath her knuckles caught on something between the floorboards. Maddie pulled out a piece of paper, a page torn from a book. She read the text, it was an historical novel, but someone had written words down the margin. Maddie read, "*I can't live like this anymore*," then heavy scribbling over some other words. She got up and felt a pause in the stirring of the room around her. She, and whatever else was there, were holding their breath.

'Bloody hell,' Maddie said aloud.

She went downstairs then and telephoned Adam at work.

'Adam, it's me.'

'Hey, how's your day off?'

'Listen, I've found something really spooky. I've been cleaning the little bedroom and there was this note under the floor. 'I can't live like this anymore."

'Well, do something else – live like what, anyway?'

'Stupid, that's what the note said. Your Gran – was she happy?'

'God knows! She was too organised to lose something under the carpet though. What are you doing anyway crawling around on the floor?'

'I said, I'm sorting out the little bedroom, but it's like someone's there with me.'

'Does this happen to all women when they get pregnant, I mean –'

'Shut up Adam. OK, talk to me about something normal.'

'Right – I'm having a chicken mayo sandwich as we speak and I think the new boss definitely fancies me.'

'Sod off, Adam, I'll see you later.'

'Bye sweetheart.'

Maddie turned from the telephone and switched on the radio quite loud. She ate a banana at the kitchen window. It was time for her doctor's appointment.

The waiting room smelt of damp cardigans and was too warm. It was the front room of a house on the main street through the village; Maddie sat down in one of the high-backed dining chairs set round the edge of the room. Like at the start of a party, she thought, the other patients were elderly and dressed in brown. Their conversations had stopped briefly as Maddie entered, but the atmosphere was not unfriendly. She had anticipated ancient copies of Woman's Own and took out her book from her bag.

'Good story, is it?' Maddie's neighbour, a sunken and wrinkled old lady with a startling purple velvet beret and one tooth, was looking at her.

'It is, yes, thank you.' It felt rude to continue to read, so Maddie closed her book and smiled at the old lady.

'I'm Maddie Parks, we've just moved into Holly Cottage.'

'Yes, I know,' the lady grinned – there were no more teeth.

The receptionist came in from her table in the hall.

'Alice Gregory, your turn now, dear.'

Maddie's companion got up; her hunched figure moved quite nimbly out of the room.

'That's our oldest resident.' Across the room, a large lady in a tight fitting coat and with enormous ankles, now spoke. Maddie imagined the receptionist returning to hand out bowls of crisps and nuts as the party got going.

'She's over a hundred years old, you know.'

'Over a hundred?' Maddie's surprise drew everyone into the conversation.

'At least a hundred and three.'

'She says she's a hundred and six.'

'Long time, eh, though?'

'Born and lived in the same house all her life.'

'Just down the road from yours.'

Maddie was glad when the receptionist called her name and she ceased to be the one in the middle with the blindfold on. But after seeing the nurse, she caught up with Alice outside the surgery.

'Have you really lived here all your life?'

'That's right – and it's a while now since I got the Queen's telegram.'

'You must have known the Dawsons in our cottage – they were my boyfriend's grandparents.'

'Oh yes, nice they were, kept themselves to themselves. And the people before that – Harris or Hazel or something, they were there a long while. Strange he was, face pressed up against the window, looking out. And then after the war, a couple and a boy, all had bright red hair. Didn't talk to anybody, although she was friendly enough.' Alice stopped.

'This is really interesting," began Maddie. "You see –'

'You must have been told about Mary Morgan?'

'Who's Mary Morgan?'

'She killed herself – in your cottage. Pretty girl, always laughing, I liked her. Told me she could do magic, would magic me a feller. Never did, though. We didn't see her then, her husband - Frank I think he was called - said she was nervous or something. Hanged herself she did. The husband stayed there till he died, shut himself away. Odd man, shifty, big ears. House was empty for a while after that.'

'My God.' Maddie sat down on the steps outside the surgery.

'It was a long time ago, you must make the house your own.' Alice put her hand on Maddie's shoulder. 'Are you hoping for a boy or a girl?'

'Um – oh – I don't mind, actually a girl I think.'

'Lovely. Well, it's nice to meet you.'

'And you.' Maddie wanted to hug the old woman for her warmth as well as the story. She felt tearful as she walked home.

Maddie found Adam's grandfather's toolbox in the cellar. She selected a heavy chisel and went upstairs to the back bedroom. No voices now but the air moved round her like a cloak circling her body. Late afternoon sunlight dipped into the room and her fair hair as she bent over the window frame, splintering the layers of white paint.

The doorbell rang downstairs and she stopped, feeling a little dizzy. George the milkman was at the front door.

'Hello, I saw you were in.'

'Hello George. Yes, I'm not working today.'

'I've got that organic juice you wanted: never been asked before, I have to say.'

'Thanks, that's great. You haven't got a minute have you, I could use some muscle?'

George blushed and followed Maddie inside and up the stairs. He hesitated outside the small bedroom. Maddie looked at him.

'This was the room where that girl –'

Maddie nodded. 'Yes, I think it was.'

'My dad was a boy when it happened. Said she was beautiful. Everyone blamed her husband, said he locked her up in here because she reckoned she could see things. Dad says everyone who lives here is a bit odd. Oh no, sorry, I didn't mean –' George blushed again and looked down at his big black boots.

Maddie laughed. 'It's OK, I'm not offended. Do you mind going in there?'

George looked up and followed her into the room. She gave him the chisel and he soon un-jammed the sash window. He was about to push it up for her but Maddie stopped him.

'I'll do it in a minute, but thank you so much. Would you like a cup of tea or a drink of something else?'

'Oh no, I'd better get back to the farm.' Once again the middle-aged bachelor farmer was embarrassed. He scratched at his unruly fair hair and was off down the stairs.

Maddie remembered she had described George to the girls at work when they had asked about the local talent. A couple of them were coming for a weekend quite soon.

She sat cross-legged on the floor and took some deep breaths.

'Mary.' She spoke the name aloud and felt the current of air slow down. Maddie sat still with her eyes closed and saw Mary in the room, reading, looking out of the window, eating off a tray. She saw a frail, dark haired young woman with lively brown eyes in a pale face, her small feet pacing the room.

'Mary, I know your story and I think I know what you're doing. You were locked in here because Frank thought you were crazy. You told him you had special powers, didn't you? And I guess that frightened him. But you have never left this house, have you?'

Maddie felt cold breath on her cheek. She still wasn't frightened, could see the small face watching her.

'You know, I'm going to be happy here with Adam and our baby.'

Maddie stood up, opened her eyes and held her hands out, feeling for the girl's shoulders.

'I'm going to open the window and I hope you feel you can leave now." Maddie heaved up the sash frame, then stood back and closed her eyes again. It took just a moment for the rush of air to brush past her and out into the open air. Maddie opened her eyes and leaned out of the window. For a while she watched the pencil grey clouds shuffle across the smudged pink sky. Someone was walking with a sheepdog across the field, she heard a bicycle bell in the lane and children's voices from the school bus. Maddie looked at her watch to see if it was late enough for something stronger than a cup of tea.

‘Fancy a drink down the pub, Mads? I see you’re ahead of me already.’ Adam had just got in and was pointing at the whisky bottle on the table.

‘I’ve only had one but yes, let’s go to the pub.’ Adam crossed the room to the stairs and Maddie followed him, putting her arms around his back.

‘I’ve got my old Adam back now and I’m so glad.’

‘Hey, what’s this?’ But he turned and they hugged.

‘Can we sit in a quiet corner? you won’t believe what happened today.’ Maddie put on a mock dramatic voice. ‘I have an incredible tale of revenge to tell you, about a woman with supernatural powers who lived in this very house.’ She stopped. ‘Actually, I sometimes wonder if I can see things like she could.’

Adam pulled away and started up the stairs. ‘For God’s sake, Maddie, don’t say that, I can’t stand loopy women. Look what happened to Mrs Rochester.’ He laughed as he walked up the stairs.

To Forty and Beyond

Do you ever think: if I hadn't done that, then that would never have happened? You know, if I hadn't missed that train, I wouldn't have been standing on the platform when the old man had the heart attack; I wouldn't have gone with him to the hospital, and talked to that nurse all that time who was having a party that night. And if I hadn't gone to the party I wouldn't have met ... that kind of thing? I do it all the time. I trace patterns in my life like the lines on a family tree. Then I rub out some so the whole structure collapses. Or the lines cross where relationships become complicated and this confuses the whole picture.

You could become screwed up about this, to the point where you daren't leave the house in case the postman delivers a certain parcel or there's an urgent telephone call. This constant analysing is a female trait apparently; litres of vodka have been consumed by girls asking why a relationship didn't work. Blokes like me are supposed to make a decision, stick to it and move on, a brief mention to your mates with the first round, then on to a discussion of Fulham's away form.

I've always been like this: I can't read a book or watch a film without imagining, what if Oliver Twist hadn't had a big appetite or Nick Hornby had supported Leyton Orient. But I had got worse as my fortieth birthday approached, noticing those first white hairs in my sideburns. I had booked the party venue: Paolo's, an expensive Italian restaurant at Fulham Broadway. They let me have the whole place that night as a thank you for all the money I had spent in there over the years. I use it for the fourth date with girlfriends: if they have survived my local pub, my cooking and meeting my mates on the first three, they deserve Paolo's. I had been through my current address book, and several old ones, and invited about a hundred friends from different parts of my life: school friends, university friends, drinking allies, work colleagues and girlfriends. Roughly even numbers in each category, I had even had proper invitations printed on nice thick, white card. None of your do-it-yourself home computer invites with something naff written on the back like 'Carl's Enterprises Ltd'.

And I had intended to go, buying a charcoal-coloured shirt from Reiss and composing a modest, witty speech during tube journeys to work. Then, a week before the party, I had gone to the Paul Klee exhibition at the Hayward Gallery. It was a warm spring afternoon, pushing for summer status with the sun a fading light bulb in a white sky. Fulham weren't at home, and after a mad, Michelob-fuelled week, I fancied an afternoon on my own. I had a Klee print above the fireplace in my bedroom and enjoyed the restful blocks of blue and orange.

The South Bank looked as ugly as ever, those grey chunks of concrete squat beside the Thames. I get lost every time I go: I think they rearrange the concrete steps and buildings every now and then to try and add mystery and interest to the architecture. Once inside the Hayward Gallery I switched off 'Tears for Fears' on my Walkman, and began the exhibition with his paintings in Tunisia. Those wonderful pictures of squares and semi circles in mustards, tangerines and sage. (My last but one girlfriend, Charlie, was a designer so I know the correct terms for these colours.) This was such a reassuring view of life, like placing the right domino one after the other. This was how I would like to see my life. I was in for a shock when I moved to Klee's later pictures – called 'Disrupted Rhythms' in the catalogue. Suddenly there were all these black lines going nowhere, bright blobs of red and yellow with no connection to anything. I sat down on a black cushioned bench, fascinated by this change in direction, so caught up in this, that I only noticed the attractive, red-haired attendant, in her uniform and official badge, as I was leaving. I emerged from the gallery into a dull afternoon; the sun's light had gone out and I was dying for a can of Coke.

Later that evening, in my flat in Hammersmith, I ordered a takeaway, turned on the TV and played the invitation responses on my answering machine. Mostly my married friends who had secured last minute babysitters, their wives had formed a 'Let's find Carl a wife' focus group. However, my mates still come out drinking on a Friday night despite Ben's chickenpox or Emily's teething. That night the combination of a Thai red curry, supermarket lager and 'Only Fools and Horses' – against the background of Klee's disturbing, disjointed pictures – set off a melancholy mood. Which is unlike me, I'm the most cheerful person I know. But I was wondering how Klee, who had seemed to have his life sorted out in his forties, could let those loose ends appear later on.

My fortieth celebration lost its appeal. What was I celebrating, if, after forty years and a series of decisions about work, friends, girlfriends, here I was on my own and as neurotic as ever? And anyway, how sad was it to buy balloons for yourself? I briefly regretted finishing with Sally, who had made it to two dates at Paolo's recently. Until I remembered her habit of folding my clothes before she joined me in bed.

I was still feeling sorry for myself on Monday morning. I categorised people on the Tube as either lonely saddos like myself or couples with intertwining briefcases. The fountain in the office foyer wasn't working and our Kylie lookalike receptionist was off sick. I work in the marketing department, and spent the morning drawing Klee-like lines on the computer. Someone brought me a coffee so I switched to screen saver, and a photograph of the Angel Falls came onto the screen. (My screen savers are either exotic locations or famous women with whom I'd like to go to these places.) I stared at this as I sipped from the plastic cup, flicked back to my Klee creations and drew a great big upturned smile. I had loads of holiday left (saved up for the MBA I was studying part-time) and I had just thought of a much better way to spend the start of my fifth decade.

I scanned the websites of Exodus Adventure and Explore Worldwide. I took Angel Falls as the sign for this next move and within two hours I was booked on a sixteen day jungle expedition in Venezuela.

So that was how I celebrated my actual birthday, canoeing to the Angel Falls with Ray and Steve and Dee and Nikki and all the others. ('Everyone joins in and you're soon amongst friends': brochure speak.) When the campfire had gone out and they were busy swapping tents, I sat in the heavy, cold night air, wrapped in a blanket, and traced the blocks in the huge rockfaces around us. I thought again of Klee's squares and parallel lines and began to deconstruct my past, moving backwards through friends, flats, jobs, girlfriends until I was back home in Middlesex with my parents again. Aeroplanes on my curtains and Fulham's cup final team above my bed, and that strained, strange Sunday lunch feeling; Gran's hearing aid buzzing and my brother Stuart helping himself to the last Yorkshire pudding. I started to rearrange the building blocks so that a different face showed. I continued this game in my head as we trekked past Indian settlements and slept in hammocks with Brazil on the horizon. As we all got browner and Ray got off with Dee and Des and Paul started bickering over breakfast, I kept coming back to the same block. As I thought of my different relationships and how they might have turned out, against each jungle setting I came up with the same face: Karen. Beautiful Karen had been my girlfriend about three years before, for about eighteen months (if you count the last month when we weren't speaking to each other.) She had gorgeous long, black hair, tight black jeans and a really dirty laugh. She had put up with the verbal agonising which accompanies my daily life: pizza or calzone, the spotty or striped tie, a flat in Hammersmith or Putney? In the clear, Evian air of South America, I reckoned I had sorted out the next piece, found the domino I should have placed three years ago.

So you know who I called up when I got back. After playing all the telephone messages: 'What happened to you, you bugger?' and 'Hey, you missed a brilliant party,' and 'Your brother's nice,' (this from Sally - poor Stuart). I assumed Karen was still working at the same place, around the corner from me in Fenchurch Street – we had frequented different wine bars since splitting up.

'Karen Crapper.' (So she hadn't got married yet; no one would keep a maiden name like that.)

'Hello Karen, it's me. It's Carl.'

'Carl, my God. I hear you missed your own party.'

'Yes, well – you didn't go then?'

''No, Ian and I were busy.'

'Ian?'

'Yes, Ian. A man who doesn't change his mind three times when ordering a bottle of wine.'

'He sounds boring.'

'Why are you calling, anyway?'

'I – well –' I saw those black jeans and purple painted toenails.

'I went away for my birthday and I've been thinking about you.'

'Mid-life crisis, is it Carl? Actually, you always were going on middle-aged. Have you still got your James Bond video collection?'

'I wish I hadn't made a mess of things.'

'You didn't make a mess, except in the bathroom. Just slept with that graduate trainee on our anniversary.' In the silence following this comment, I could see Karen twisting the end of her ponytail.

'Can we meet for a drink? I've got one hell of a suntan.'

I don't think my suntanned body was what did it, but she agreed in the end, and we met the following evening in Paolo's. Karen looked stunning. She had her hair up but sort of falling down her neck, like shiny black feathers. The tightly fitting dark green dress I took as a good sign.

'Where do you keep your knuckle dusters in that outfit?'

'What? Oh, don't tell me, your name is Bond, James Bond. Still got that tatty leather jacket, I see.'

Two glasses of wine later, I heard that amazing laugh again.

'So, I was the only celibate member of the expedition. Imagine that?'

'No, I can't. You haven't got a girlfriend, then?'

My mate Marco the waiter brought us a second bottle of wine.

Karen had ordered the house red before I could even open the wine list. I changed the subject.

'Do you go to art galleries with this Ian?'

'Sometimes, why?' As Karen took a mouthful of pasta, I watched how her dress zip ran from under one arm down her side; it was a big turn on (and was holding out well following bruschetta and a huge bowl of linguine).

'There's this exhibition of Klee's –'

'Yes, I've been. You've got a picture of his at the end of your bed.' And she blushed the colour of sundried tomatoes at letting this bit of memory slip out.

'What did you think?'

'Nice colours, a bit repetitive. I liked his last ones, though. More freedom of expression, less contrived I think.'

We chatted through another bottle of red wine and a couple of grappas (or is it grappae?) Karen's hazel eyes had become as black as her glossy hair, her dark eye make-up was a bit smudged; she looked incredible and to think she used to live with me. She was talking about herself now.

'I want a baby, Carl.' Just like that, without any build up. 'Unlikely as it seems, I'm willing to trade figure-hugging jeans for maternity leggings.'

We held hands across the table, hugged before she got into a taxi at Fulham Broadway. I'm pretty sure I said, 'You know, I think you're the one,' but that night I went over our conversations so often, it might have been wishful thinking. Was this it, then? Had I at last made the right decision: here was Karen wanting a family and here was I trying to make sense of my life. I should have felt chuffed at sorting myself out. Instead I felt I had flopped down onto a big, cosy cushioned sofa – and couldn't get up again.

It was funny, we bumped into each other the next day at lunchtime. Three years of working so close and this was the first time it had happened. It was a windy day, I was trying to carry a takeaway coffee, a baguette and a newspaper. Karen's hair was loose and kept cutting across her mouth as she spoke. We were both stuck between the memory of the previous evening and not knowing what to do with it. She said she would call me at the weekend, put her arms round me in a funny way. That afternoon a friend on my MBA course asked if I wanted to go out for a drink. Jenny's a good laugh, we arranged to meet after work outside my office. It was great to put all this forty and a bit soul-searching aside. We had a few beers and a Mexican in Covent Garden and I lent Jenny my leather jacket as the wind had turned really nasty by midnight. On the tube journey home I thought again of Karen, hoping for a warm, comforting glow to warm me up (missing my leather jacket). Instead I felt smothered rather than sorted; a bit stuffed, too, after the enchiladas. I closed my eyes and woke just in time for Hammersmith station.

Karen phoned first thing on Saturday morning.

'Carl, it's me, Karen.'

'You didn't used to get up this early.'

'Carl, did you read my note?' Laid back Karen sounded tense, she would definitely be fiddling with her hair.

'What note?'

'I – actually, I don't think it matters. This is all a bit awkward, isn't it? I mean, we did finish before, and for a bloody good reason. And here you are again –'

'Sorry, Karen, I'm not with you, here I am what?'

'Just because we had a nice evening, but – why would it work this time? You like to sleep with the windows open, I sleep with the windows closed. That sort of thing.'

'Karen, I feel like my bookmark is half way through a novel but I don't remember starting the story. What *are* you talking about?'

'Paul Simon. Post Art Garfunkel. I've got some uncool albums, too. Never mind. It just seems mad to even think about going through all this again.'

I didn't say anything, I needed some breakfast before this sort of conversation.

'I might as well tell you, Carl. I waited outside your office yesterday and you met some girl. And – well, I know we're not going out or anything. But I'm going to stay with Ian because at least I can trust him.'

'Oh Karen, I –'

'Bye, Carl.'

I walked to the fridge and drank from the carton of orange juice. I had been incredibly selfish, not thinking about Karen trying to sort out her own course in life. Which I had crossed and, by doing so, had created a knot.

Jenny dropped off my leather jacket a bit later. Just in time as I was about to leave for Craven Cottage. I locked the door and put the key in my pocket. And found the note. The one Karen had been talking about. I sat on my doorstep and read: 'I think you're the one, too.' So that was what that strange hug was all about, she must have put it in my pocket then. Where on earth does that fit in with the scheme of things? Apart from in some Thomas Hardy novel.

I didn't go and watch Fulham, I went back to the Klee exhibition. It was raining this time and they had moved the staircase again. I headed straight for the last paintings. Because if you're trying to live logically, as with his neatly stacked blocks and carefully drawn lines, how do you make sense of my not finding that note? Karen could be standing holding my hand right now if I hadn't lent my jacket to Jenny. And Jenny wouldn't have called me if her boyfriend hadn't finished with her and she needed cheering up. This was much bigger than the old man on the platform and nurse's party scenario (yes, that *was* me). And so it goes on. That note was pure Klee at the end, and there it was in one of the paintings: a yellow blob suspended in mid air. My life brought to a stop with a big, bright blob of paint. But this time, instead of missing the lines connecting it back to anything, I looked at the spaces in between and saw them as opportunities ahead. I would probably still agonise over whether I caught the right train or left the pub too early, but I would not regret the decision once it was made.

Big thoughts for a Saturday afternoon. I turned on my Walkman as I left, to catch the half time scores.

Maude Fairwell's House

Maude selected 'House and Garden' from the magazines and stretched herself along Mrs Goodman's new cream sofa. Two hours at least before Mrs Goodman returned from her shopping in town, and Maude had already dusted and hoovered downstairs, and washed the windows. The spring sunshine fell through the gleaming panes of glass and warmed the floral cushions behind her shoulders. She admired the gloss of the polished mirror over the fireplace, stroked her hand along the sofa's expensive covers and read about ivory as the new white in interior design.

She stretched herself then got up, went over to her reflection in the fireplace mirror. She straightened the plum-coloured velvet hat over her thick grey curls. The hat had been hanging in the hall and matched the cardigan she was wearing. Maude wondered if Mrs Goodman had the same shade in a lipstick: it would be in the little padded box on the dressing table upstairs. She scratched at a smudge of dust on her plump, round face, quite pink from the warmth of the house, and headed for the kitchen. She picked up the rubber gloves and, before putting them on, sprinkled in the Crabtree & Evelyn lavender talcum powder she had found in one of the bathrooms. Maude's gloved hand tuned the radio from Radio 4 to Magic FM and picked up the Dettox spray.

Half an hour later Mrs Goodman's oak kitchen cupboards were waxed to a glow. Maude had given the fridge a thorough clean, too, removing a yoghurt past its sell-by date. She also took out some Danish Blue and a pack of smoked salmon. Her foot flipped up the lid on the pedal bin, she dropped in the yoghurt and her shoe hovered whilst she smelled again the cheese and salmon. The lid fell on the bin as she wrapped these two items in a polythene bag from one of the kitchen drawers. She slipped this into her large handbag by the front door.

Whilst in the hall she noticed the black binliner, destined for a charity shop, which Mrs Goodman had forgotten to take with her into town. Maude dragged the bag across the parquet floor and lowered herself onto the stairs. She pulled out an assortment of paperbacks, tea towels, blouses and household objects.

'Surely she's not getting rid of this?' Maude asked aloud as she held up a mauve silk shirt. She had seen Mrs Goodman wearing it not long ago in church. She found a split in the seam under the arm, and thought of her sewing machine back home.

She pulled herself up on the banister rail and refilled the binliner. She tucked the shirt into her bag, along with a leather spectacles case and some silver plated napkin rings. Maude was thinking of her niece's wedding next month. The brass candle holder didn't fit so she lay this across the top of the bag.

She returned to the kitchen. The Bee Gees had faded out on the radio and the eleven o'clock news was announced. She peeled off her gloves and turned on the kettle. The usual tray of teabags, digestives and smiley face mug was on the butcher's block. Maude ignored these and reached up for the Crown Derby teapot and matching cup and saucer from the dresser. The Earl Grey was in its usual place and there were still some of those continental wafer biscuits left. The tray replenished, she returned to the sofa.

Maude was slowly dipping the dark chocolate wafer in her tea when she heard the thud against the back door. She was too warm amongst the cushions to move, but the shattering of glass caused her tea to spill as she heaved her large frame into action.

'Who's there?' Maude picked up the solid glass ashtray from the coffee table and held this above her head as she marched into the kitchen.

'Daniel Cartwright, what on earth do you think you're doing?'

A tall, skinny teenager stood just inside the back door, staring at his right hand which was bleeding from several cuts across his knuckles.

'For heaven's sake, you're dripping all over my nice clean floor.' Maude put down the ashtray and grabbed the boy by his wrist.

'Ow, get off! What are you going to do?'

‘I’m going to wash those cuts, you silly boy,’ and she pulled him by the arm to the sink. She held tight onto his wrist and turned on the tap, maintaining her grip despite his moans as the cold water sliced into the cuts.

‘Now, can I trust you to sit on that chair and don’t move whilst I find you some Savlon?’

Daniel stared at Maude as he wrapped his hand in the tea towel she had given him.

‘Mrs Fairwell, I thought you lived in my grandad’s road.’

‘I still do, stupid boy. And I know where you live as well, so no running off.’

Maude returned with some antiseptic cream and a bandage.

‘I don’t need that, it’s fine now.’ Daniel began to get up.

‘You sit down, young man.’ And Daniel sat whilst she bandaged his hand, then watched, as she swept up the glass from the broken pane in the door, and washed the floor. The Shadows strummed on the radio. Maude fetched the plate of digestives and put them in front of him on the table.

‘Eat one of these, you look a bit pale.’

Daniel shook his head and wiped his nose on his sweatshirt cuff. Maude sat down opposite him.

‘So. Are you going to tell me what you were doing - or shall I take you straight to the police station?’

Daniel’s face went a shade lighter, he picked up a biscuit and broke it in half.

‘Please don’t tell the police, can’t you say it was an accident? I’ll pay for the glass and everything.’

‘Why were you breaking in, Daniel?’

‘It was for a laugh, a bet with my mates. They said Mrs Goodman is always out on a Friday and she leaves a key under a flowerpot. But the key wasn’t there. I wasn’t going to take anything, it was just – just to see if I could get in.’

‘The key wasn’t there because I use it to get in. So you came round the back and -?’

‘I didn’t mean to break the glass. I saw the key in the keyhole and sort of tapped at the pane and the next minute –’

Daniel flattened biscuit crumbs into the table top, not looking at the stone grey eyes watching him. Maude knew Daniel and his family as she knew everyone in the village. Daniel's family didn't go to church, and his mother, who worked in the corner shop, had short-changed her last week. Mr Fairwell spent far too long every Saturday lunchtime, playing dominoes in the Swan with Daniel's grandfather.

'Daniel Cartwright, I don't know what I should do with you. I'm going to have to think about it.'

'You're not going to tell, are you? My Mum will be mad.'

'I think you should go now, Mrs Goodman will be back soon. I haven't decided what I'm going to do.'

Daniel frowned at Maude as he got up.

'I'd go out of the front if I was you, there may still be glass at the back.' Daniel looked at Maude and then ran out of the kitchen and into the hall. But she didn't hear the door open. Instead, walking more slowly this time, Daniel returned to the kitchen.

'Is that your bag in the hall, Mrs Fairwell?'

'What? Yes, it is – why?'

'And all those things in it: they're yours?'

'Of course they are. Now can you go, I've got some cleaning –'

'It just seems a bit strange. Why would anyone walk around with candlesticks and clothes and God knows what else stuffed into their bag. Does Mrs Goodman know you've got them?'

'You impertinent ... how dare you! I'm not the one who broke into her house and –'

'No, but I didn't steal anything, did I?'

Daniel stood with his hands on his hips, staring at Maude from underneath his long fringe. It was she who looked down now.

'So, I think you know what you're going to say about the accident, don't you? You broke the glass with the broom handle when you were sweeping the floor, didn't you?'

Maude's hands were busy tidying the crumbs on the table into a neat little pile.

'Well, Mrs Fairwell?'

She looked up, her face a bruised apple showing shadows of grey instead of her usual plump, pink complexion.

'Right, I'll be off then.' Daniel grinned this time before heading for the hall. Maude heard the door open.

'Oh, Mrs Fairwell,' he called through to her. 'I'm sure the hat looks better on her.'

The front door closed. She got up, tipped the handful of crumbs into the dustbin, refilled the kettle and turned up the radio. She hummed along to Neil Sedaka as she took down another teacup from the dresser.

'One more cuppa then I'll start upstairs,' she said aloud. Mrs Goodman always praised Maude's cleaning and paid her generously. She said Maude was the most efficient cleaning lady she had ever had.

POETRY & SHORT PROSE

High Summer Sky

In the sky a satellite
Beamed the rest of the world
Back to him. In the sky he saw
Pale blue mornings
Children going to school.
The blue arch spread over summer picnics and
Sleeping in the sun. Clouds curling across the
High summer sky, sail boats
Swell across water.
His hands curl around the bars,
Blue is space, laughter, the colour of outside
With no edges or walls.
A parachute tugging at the shadows behind him.

High Grass

Through high grass right to the ends of the earth.
The height and heat of the sun
Stretches the day to its ends.
She walks through the grass towards the edge.
Dry yellow grass, brittle in the summer heat
Scratching her white skirt and pale legs.
A box of matchsticks squared up on a mantelpiece.
The grass cracks and flattens as she sits,
The hood of blue sky pulls over her.
Muffled insect sounds in the grass
Now scrape and snap next to her head.
A hairbrush of stalks scours her feet.
Fair hair striped against straw.
She looks across the field,
An expanse of mustard yellow reaching to the edge,
The flag of blue above.

Yellow

My favourite wine gum glows,
Streetlights ignite the dark,
The linen suit I wore to your wedding.
The warning traffic light,
My anger's burning oil,
The roses in your buttonhole and her bouquet.
The fire now warms and melts,
Sherbet lemons fizzing,
Your matching rings chimed the flutes with gold.
Camomile tea and lemon curd
Soothe with Coldplay's mellow song.
They'll be drinking pina coladas now
In the last liquid sunlight.

Antigua Sea

The early empty horizon sea
Is turquoise blue stained glass.
A delicate smile
To the late afternoon's
Bold laughter
Of deep sapphire blue.
Later still the
Glassy icy black of midnight.

The waves whooped all night,
Subdued to a hush
In the wide, white early morning.
But with heavy afternoon's heat
The sea's teasing skirt
Spreads a white lace hem of spray.
Smoothed onto the sand
Then hitched up again.

I swam at midnight.
The sharp blackness was not icy
But a soft, lapping liquid.
The warmth of black coffee
Dappled by milk from the moon.

Tea

Ticking timepiece tilts the time
Towards three
And teatime.
One not two teacups and
Teabag not teapot
On the old tin tea tray,
Trams and trains from their
Trip on a steam train
Tinged with tangerine teastain rings.
Threadbare trousered thin knees
Tip against the teak table
As trembling hands transfer the tray.
He takes a Tesco's Rich Tea
No more toasted teacakes
And treacle tart,
Homemade treats
From when there were two of them.
Two teacups, a teapot, a tablecloth
And talk and touching knees
At teatime.

Carsington

Christmas in London:
Loud laughter under low ceilings,
Oversized packaging in undersized rooms,
Coats, bags and empty bottles tripping up in narrow halls.

The journey away was already planned,
Cases packed, the sky was a holiday blue.

A farmhouse in Derbyshire:
It stood with its back to the road.
Long windows showed us the wide, hard clodded fields
Falling away between low limestone walls,
Down to the distant grey silk lake.
Sun's apricot bloom behind dark branches,
Like a pink rose outlined in the lattices of a window.

Inside the house:
A basket of logs, a bowl of fresh eggs,
The fire lit and toast made, eggs scrambled a rich yellow.
The night wound itself round the house,
Our sleep was muffled by the dark outside,
Softer here above the silent fields,
Spreading across the drowsy earth to the silver plated lake.

In the morning
From the cold, thick walled window-sill,
The lake now a pale blue saucer on a white cotton tablecloth,
The silence had been sealed by a fall of snow.
Thick socks on the flagstone floor,
Fried eggs, coffee then the sharp blue air,
The whole breadth of outside spun to the horizon by the snow.

The lake a sheet of blue metal
Hammered between the trees.

Dusty Old Box

I left him a fork and a dusty old box
Knowing he was a cunning old fox.
I hoped his eyes would gaze beyond
The weedy fringes of the pond.
No luck! It seemed his eye was stuck on me,
Critically dissecting, embarrassing, he
Wouldn't lose that penetrating stare
That pounded and grinded me into its snare.
Pulling away quickly, I seized the dog's lead
But on it he simply just trod on and peed.
I picked it up and realised too late
The cake had a mouse in it and I dropped the plate.

I left him a fork and a dusty old box,
What would he do, the cunning old fox?
I had hoped his eyes would gaze beyond
The green, weedy fringes of the pond.
But his eyes threw and pinned a stare onto me
Critically dissecting, mocking, and he
Held me too still and too close with that stare
That pounded and grinded me into its snare.
Pulling away quickly, I seized the dog's lead,
His leg caught, he stood on it, growled and then peed.
The dog and I moved but the eyes had now gone
I could see the old box on the edge of the pond.
I pulled back the flaps and realised too late
The cake was just dust and I dropped the plate.

Public Records Office, Kew

Kew Bridge
In a sharp cold breeze;
Hands curled up coat sleeves,
Shoes tapping the pavement and
Leather gloved fingertips tapping the wheel.
No time to look
At the green, grey Thames
A slow bulk below the bridge.

The building in Kew:
Seventies slabs of concrete.
The cold and hurry parked outside,
Mobile phone calls and chatter
Left with the coffee cups and cakecrumbs.

Silence
Behind the glass walls.
Movements slow down,
Pencilled words crawl across notepads,
A pair of white gloves smooth a page corner.
A hushed respect
For those old distant secrets
Bound within new concrete covers.

A Monologue of Annoyance

I hate it when he does that, she thought, always saying the wrong thing at the wrong time. Such a beautiful afternoon and he's ruined it. I know we've not been getting on, but ... This should be the perfect Sunday afternoon, handsome thirty-something couple that we are, taking a walk by the river. Feeling nice and hazy after the cider in the pub, like the golden hazy sunlight between the trees and on the river.

She recalled their arguing that morning, usual stuff, his dirty football kit still soaking in the bath, bits of sideburn clogging the basin while she cleaned her teeth, no milk or juice in the fridge. And when she asked if he could manage a visit to Tesco's ... He yelled, she yelled, he went for a paper and, not for the first time, she wondered if he might not come back.

So now they're walking by the river, elbows bumping rather than hands holding, crossing the dusty paths and muted conversations of other couples. Sunday afternoons should stretch ahead like the long shadows of the dark trees and the flow of the river, she thought. But not now, not after what he had just said. She looked down at the slices of sunlight cutting into the water and wondered how to reply. He repeated his question: "Will you marry me?"

The Rocking Chair

The rocking chair in my parents' sitting room, in the corner. The syrup varnish spread on the wood is worn in places. Between these spoonfuls the wood is lighter, duller. The wood feels smooth where sleeves rest along the length of the arms. The lines in the wood are map contours, tracing a route around the chair. The joints are darker, black treacle poured into the cracks. I used to scratch my thumbnail in between these joints. The high back loops behind the head then stretches into the arms. They become the curls of a treble clef; curling to their arm ends which are smooth, round pebbles in the palm of the hand.

It is elegant and homely, a graceful woman with a straight back, filling the teapot and swaying in time to music.

There are two or three cushions on the chair, my mother made these from old clothes and curtains. A green and orange flowered dress my mother wore to church: I am sat in her lap. Our beautiful black cat slept here with his tail tucked in. The rocker was still, our cat brought silence to the room. As children, we made the rocking chair sail, the skirting boards were knocked and there was a dent cut into my parents' old-fashioned stippled wallpaper. As the chair sat in the same place, the rocking chair always nudged the same part of the wall.

The chair did not move when my father sat there and read his newspaper, anchored by the rockers. Gran used to visit on Sundays and she liked to sit in the rocking chair. She didn't read, she was just there. Her feet did just touch the floor, I'm sure her toes tipped the chair to and fro. She fell asleep, head forward, hands tucked in like the cat's tail. I would like to be old in a rocking chair on a porch in Massachusetts, the scratched skirting boards my clapboard house behind me. Watching people walk home from work, and beyond, always a view of the sea.

The proceeds generated by the sale of this book are to be donated to the charity Cancer Active. Their aim is to lay out all the relevant information on cancer prevention and care so that no one need die of ignorance. They do not judge or choose between therapies but endeavour to cover the full spectrum of possible therapies so that informed choices can be made (ranging from surgery to supplements, radiotherapy to reiki, chemotherapy to ozone therapy, the very best of orthodox and complementary treatments).

Their mission is to thoroughly research the facts and then present them in an easy to understand way.
They are independent and promise that their opinions are unbiased.

Their simple belief, born out of many scientific studies, is that cancer is a disease of the whole body, not merely a lump localised in a particular organ. As such, the best chance of beating it - or preventing it - is through a whole body solution, (an holistic solution), an integrated package of therapies that would incorporate the most effective elements known to health professionals. Since there is no one, single disease called cancer – a patient's cancer is as individual as he or she is - they will need someone to help them prepare a personal programme. Another of the aims of the charity is to help in this process.

They have already started to develop programmes on healthy eating, immune system building and cancer prevention for schools. Tests have already taken place on lessons to add to the curriculum. They won't just be educating on foods but, for example, on sexual diseases that cause cancer, on the dangers from toxins in lipsticks or anti-perspirants, or from mobile phones or smoking.

Laws on supplements are passed because Governments and interested parties are organised. The opposition is not.

Toxins abound in our environment because the businesses that use the toxic ingredients are highly professional. The opposition is not.

Despite worrying research for eight or more years, HRT has 2.2 million daily users at risk because the pharmaceutical PR is disciplined. The opposition is not.

Therefore, another aim is to lead the organisation of the opposition. They aim to organise the people who care, be they University Professors, students, health practitioners or ordinary people in the street. They intend to lobby journalists, governments and everybody who influences and makes decisions.